THE **ACCOUNTANTS**

The Accountants

A NOVEL

BRENDAN JOHN LEE

ISBN: 978-0-473-66192-2
Edition 2.0

Preface

You could say accounting is in my blood. I got the gene from my mother. It was my best subject in high school. It was my major at university. I graduated and went straight into an accounting firm. I didn't last long from there. After four years as a tax accountant, I left to pursue something new. That 'new' ended up being travel writing, which is still my career today.

It's always struck me as interesting, though, that despite over a decade away from the profession I was never able to shed my accounting skin. To my friends, I am still their 'accountant friend'. Whenever I meet someone new, I always get an "Ahh!" when the accountant part of my story comes up. It's as if nothing about me makes sense without it.

However, during the many long bus and plane rides I've since been on, I think back to that part of my life often, and it's started making sense to me, too. My short life as an accountant shaped who I am. Those years were some of the best and worst of my life. The worst, because I knew it was not where I wanted to be. The best, because of the wonderful friendships I made, which I still cherish all these years later.

Those friendships inspired this book. It was the characters I met during those years that made the job both bearable and memorable. Accountants are unique people, sure, but not in the way most people imagine. Of course, *The Accountants* is entirely fictional, but each character is inspired by a real person or persons. Much of the dialogue is also inspired by real conversations, as best as I can remember them.

One interesting thing I noticed about my fellow accountants – none of us ever grew up wanting to be accountants, unlike many doctors or lawyers or pilots. Every one of us had dreams of being somewhere else or doing something else. Sometimes, it felt like that was all we ever talked about. But that ended up being a good thing. We talked so often about all the other great places we could be; some of us actually ended up getting there.

Early in 2020, at the start of the Covid-19 pandemic lockdowns, I undertook a writing challenge to complete a novel in four weeks. I knew to have any chance of success, I needed to write about a place or people I knew intimately, where words would flood effortlessly onto the page. Interestingly, my head went not to my hobbies or passions, but to accounting. What came out was a story about many things – an accountant's life, sure, but also friendship, love, purpose, identity, and the importance of *living*.

I love *The Accountants*. I hope you will too. I know some paragraphs might be 'accountants only', but in the end it's a book about taking a chance, understanding it's never too late, and chasing what's in your heart while you still can – and I know that is universal.

With love,
B.

THE ACCOUNTANTS

To those who had the courage to chase a dream.

To those who were taken from us before they could.

Prologue

I open my eyes. For a moment, I forget where I am. Then I see my dirty feet, the empty wine bottle sitting beside them, my phone on the reception coffee table. I laugh.

You forgot you were *here*? How?

I sit up and look for a clean patch on my sleeve to wipe my eyes. Moonlight floods in through the floor-to-ceiling window in front of me. I check the time.

3:41 a.m.

That's when I notice the couch beside me is empty. Where's Sienna?

I turn my head to the boardroom and whisper her name. Again. Three times. Nothing.

Strange.

I peel myself off the couch, shuffle to the window. Seven storeys below, my eyes flick between the flashing blue and red lights, the news cameras, the men in suits talking on radios. I look at the park I used to walk across every morning, now patrolled by officers holding rifles. I'm reminded of those late nights at the office, when the clock started creeping towards midnight and we used to joke that we might as well sleep here.

Look at us now.

Then I remember. Sienna. Need to find Sienna.

I go to the lunchroom. It looks empty at first, and my stomach drops, but as I look closer I see the boys against the far wall, asleep on the floor.

Good. But no Sienna.

I tip toe back to reception. In the semi-darkness, my eyes scan the room. The couches. The desk. The elevators. All looks normal. Then I glance towards the door to the stairwell. It's still blocked with the pile of desks and chairs we stacked against it. I squint, look closer. It looks different. I'm not sure how, it just does. But as I walk towards it, I can tell – someone's been here. And then a *thump-thump-thump* starts to echo from my ribcage as I see the door to the stairwell, the door we're supposed to stay away from, the door that should never be opened, is open.

That's when I knew it was just a matter of time. All of us were going to die.

Part 1

We always talked about it like it was the worst place in the world. And we always laughed when we did, but we were never joking. We didn't see the irony that we were a part of that place as much as everybody else; if it were the worst place in the world, that would have made us some of the world's worst people. And of course, we didn't believe *that* to be true. How could we? When we worked so hard and dressed so well and never called in sick, except when it was raining particularly badly, or our throats were sorer than usual. We didn't realise it at the time, but in a way, we all grew up in that place – it's where we got our first real salary, had our first client meetings, for some of us, it was the first place we ever wore a tie. They say you never get to choose your family, and that's what makes them special. I guess they weren't just talking about mothers, fathers and siblings because in that office, none of us got to choose each other either – we just showed up one day, and there we were. And we didn't plan it this way, but for those years, we spent more time with each other than we did with our real families. We said we hated it. Somehow, we loved it too. I guess in between all the Monday morning cursing and pledges to leave and never come back, it was somehow lost on us, how the worst place in the world could end up creating some of our best memories.

Monday

The office of Grant & Woodson stood on a corner. It was the last corner, on the last street, on the forgotten north end of Auckland city. A concrete seven-storey building – one that looked deceptively ugly and weathered on the outside – and I say 'deceptively' because on the inside it was rather spick and new. It was the tallest building for four blocks, nothing special, of course, compared to the forty-storey skyscrapers that clustered along Queen Street and the waterfront. But it was the pride of this little bubble, on this little corner, on this little end of town.

The building was diverse; on the ground floor – the Pride of Persia restaurant where we liked to eat lunch on rainy days, on the second and third floors – the regional office of some insurance company, the fourth floor was the physiotherapy clinic, the fifth floor was the architects, and on the sixth and seventh floors were us.

It was apparently quite a story, Grant & Woodson, started by a couple of rag-tag accountants up north in Whangarei, who over the seventies and eighties had grown their pint-sized consultancy, clients of mostly cafes and fish-and-chip shops, into one of the largest accounting firms in the country. There was even a plaque in reception of a prestigious entrepreneurship award they'd won some years back. None of us actually knew who Mr Grant and Mr Woodson were or what they looked like, if those were, in fact, their real names, or if they were even real people. Not that it would have been hard to find out, just none of us had ever cared enough to do so. All we knew was Mr Grant and Mr Woodson weren't here anymore, at least not in this office. Grant & Woodson now consisted of five divisions and sixteen partners, none of whom were named Grant or Woodson.

There was one partner named Drewlove, though. Sam Drewlove, and I knew him rather well because he was the partner I worked for. Before I was hired as a graduate, I had been to the office for three interviews and never seen Sam Drewlove once. When

I showed up for my first day of work – I was a scrappy young man then, in a brand new suit and a three-month-old haircut – I was told I'd be working in Mr Drewlove's team and wondered why I'd never seen or heard of this man before. But it wasn't hard to guess why once I met him.

I guess you could say Sam Drewlove wasn't the most exciting man. Divorced, and not ugly but not handsome, Sam Drewlove was a thin, short man, with a sad moustache and a high-pitched voice. He had five plain-coloured suits he wore in the same specific order each week – brown, navy, black, light grey, dark grey – each with its own shirt and tie. The shirts were always too big, his sleeves ballooned out like a jester's, though my guess was he liked them that way. If you had to compare his face to an animal, the obvious choice would be a mouse, or maybe a guinea pig, with small eyes that were kind of close together, and a thin nose that pointed slightly to the left. He was a harmless man, Sam Drewlove, and wickedly intelligent, but his temperament irritated you just enough that when you entered a room with him, all you thought about was how long you had left until you could leave.

Now, in my third year, my relationship with Sam Drewlove had evolved somewhat. It started neutral, but he was unpredictable, and his mood changed constantly. Yet they were gradual, month-to-month changes, rather than changes by the day. Some seasons, it felt like he was trying too hard to be my friend, my *bro*, coming to my desk with a jolly smile, asking me about the weekend and my girlfriend and the latest NBA game, even though he knew nothing about what I did on weekends, or basketball, or my girlfriend. And then at the same pace the weather turned, he morphed into the passive-aggressive, overbearing school teacher, calling me into his office to scold me about being five minutes late, even though I always stayed after hours anyway; or that my fees were lower than last month, even though we always billed more than every other team in the office.

I suppose, for Sam Drewlove, even though he took home nearly a million dollars a year, he spent fourteen hours a day in that office and went home to an empty house each night. We were the closest thing he had to a family. But we were also his livelihood. That meant he had to balance good-copping-bad-copping between us, though we all felt he did a miserable job of it, and it just annoyed us more than anything.

When I walked into the office eleven minutes late on this particular morning, Sam Drewlove was in his overbearing season. It was August then, the cold mornings often leaving him more irritable than usual.

7

Please see me when you arrive.

The email had been sent at 8:29. As I trudged across the office, past the managers' cubicles at least three times the size of my own, I tried to think of a good excuse, but August didn't like me much either; it was one of those mornings where the only thing you wanted to do was unplug your phone and log off your email, not see or talk to anybody, and hope things got better by lunch.

I poked my head in the door. "Wanted to see me?"

"Yes. Hi. I called you at 8:30. You weren't at your desk."

I wanted to say, 'You sent your email at 8:29, which means you probably called me at 8:28, which means you really couldn't have known if I was at my desk at 8:30 or not, unless of course you had left your office and come over to look, which I highly doubt and would gladly put money on it, I'm that sure.' But I didn't.

"Just had a little trouble at home this morning."

"Nothing serious I hope."

I could hear the eye roll in his voice. "Nobody's dying, if that's what you're asking."

He crossed his legs, swung his chair to face me. "We start work at 8:30 for a reason. Business starts at 8:30. I was here at 6:30, and I needed to talk to you, but I didn't call you at 6:30. I waited until 8:30. If I call you at 8:30, you should be here. That's the whole reason I have staff, so you're there when I need you to do something."

"It was just today. I'll be here at 8:29 tomorrow."

He looked at me blankly, wondering if I was making a joke. "Anyway," he said dismissively, as if I were a delinquent son he was dealing with only because he had no choice. "This is the file on Fetherby. He came back with those numbers we asked for. Update everything, then get Peter to refile this with the IRD. Today. Please."

I took the file and turned to walk out.

"And will you tell Gordon to see me? Now. Please."

Of course, by Gordon, he meant my good friend Chocolate. Chocolate hadn't been there when I'd arrived and still wasn't there when I got back to my desk. I guessed he was getting a coffee, or having a cigarette, or both. He rolled around the corner five minutes later, smelling of cigarette smoke with a steaming cup in his hand.

"Boss wants to see you."

"About what?"

"Wants to take you ice skating? How would I know?"

He set his coffee down and peered across the top of the cubicles towards Drewlove's office, as if scoping out an enemy target. "Far, is that a new shirt?" he said, looking back down at me. He pulled at my collar, flicking it against my face. "Shucks bro, that silk or something?" He laughed. "You get a pay rise or something?"

"Don't be jealous."

"Jealous, bro, *you* better be jealous, little ol' Sam Drewlove calling me into his office, probably about to give me a pay rise right now. Shucks, why else would he need to see the Chocolate man?"

I watched Chocolate walk across the office, shoulders high like he was bracing for a ribbing. For some reason we always felt like that, getting called into that office. Even though it happened five or six times a day, and most times it was nothing – he was just handing back a job or asking about a client – over time, you just conditioned yourself for the worst. Though it did seem Chocolate clashed with Drewlove more than the rest of us.

Gordon Knightley was a year ahead of me at Grant & Woodson, and wasn't your usual suspect of a senior accountant. A light-skinned Samoan, he'd grown up in a large, single-father household, just on the skirts of South Auckland. Not many accountants tended to come out of South Auckland, some of the high schools down there didn't even bother offering it as a subject, but he'd found an affinity to numbers that led him to the subject in university and now a full-time desk here at lucky Grant & Woodson. Of course, the boss always called him by his real name, Gordon, but the rest of us called him Chocolate, to quote his oft-told stories, 'all the girls in Thailand' used to call him that, so we all started calling him that too. One time, his sister came to the office to meet him for lunch, and we overheard her say as the elevator doors closed, 'Did that guy just call you Chocolate?' Nobody outside the office called him Chocolate, only we did, and if they heard us say it, they didn't know why. Some thought the nickname came from the daily Peanut Slabs he ate from the office vending machine; a logical guess, but not close at all. We guessed those Thailand stories were just for us, and maybe they weren't even true. Didn't matter, we started calling him Chocolate, and he never minded, so we never stopped.

Even if I hadn't been overjoyed to be put in Sam Drewlove's team, I decided it wasn't so bad when I got sat next to Chocolate Knightley on my first day. He was older, but not that much older, and senior, but not that much more senior, so he didn't have to act like a boss, and I didn't have to act like I took my job any more seriously than I did. I quickly learned at Grant & Woodson there was always a balance of power being played between the bosses and the people – the East Side and the West Side – and as staff got older and more senior, they started to move onto the side of the bosses. But for now, Chocolate was still on the side of the people.

Chocolate and I becoming good friends was a welcome blessing in my life because he wasn't the usual person I'd become friends with. My first friend from South Auckland, and my only friend from South Auckland, not because South Auckland was full of terrible people – it wasn't – but simply because I never had a reason to go out there and never did. You would never know from looking at him, but I found out some weeks after meeting him that Chocolate had a drip of Chinese in him, too, a Chinese great grandfather who had fled to Samoa back before the war. He didn't know anything about him, not even a name, and that surprised me at first until I realised nobody really knows anything about their great grandfathers, including myself. But he shared the one or two stories he did know, like the time he got a red packet on Chinese New Year from a distant cousin he never saw again, and how the first Chinese restaurant in Apia was actually started by his family line, though nobody could actually prove it. But the biggest blessing of becoming friends with Chocolate was, he was my neighbour in that office, and while I hadn't realised it when we shook hands on the first day, we were at those desks five, six, sometimes seven days a week. Overnight, he had become the person in my life I spent more time with than anybody, and I couldn't imagine what life would have been like had I sat next to someone who hadn't become a friend but simply stayed a stranger, or even become an enemy.

Chocolate and I had such different upbringings it was hard to believe we grew up in the same city sometimes. He was well-built and suave, I was short and ordinary; I grew up cushy and upper-middle-class, he grew up not dirt-poor, but certainly not rich either. One day we were watching a video of two kids fighting outside a school on his computer, and he told me of the time his high school and another high school had organised a big fight by the rugby fields one afternoon like they often did. Someone got stabbed in the arm, and his friend got knocked out with a pole from an uprooted road sign. Police showed up not two hours late, but two days late, questioning a couple of kids and arresting nobody. Chocolate recited it with such normalcy I knew he wasn't exaggerating. I hadn't even known that kind of thing happened in New Zealand. Compared to my school days; the most traumatic thing I could remember was somebody stealing my umbrella one freezing afternoon and having to walk to the bus stop in the rain.

Of course, even now, with his 'good' job and life together, life wasn't a dance in the park for Chocolate. After drinking too many Lion Reds on Friday nights, his stories always came out, about his dad still drinking, or his brother needing money *again*, or his ex-fiancé, the one with whom he had a six-year-old son, the one he seemed to fight with over text message every hour of every day, the one he paid 'more and more child support every year' yet she 'still had no money for rugby boots'. Maybe that's the real reason I liked Chocolate. He was a father; I was still a kid. He had lots of stories, I had none. Polar opposites, which meant friendship was easy from the beginning.

"Same old bullshit," he mumbled as he walked behind me back to his desk.

"What happened?" I rolled my chair around to his cubicle, sure to grab a file off my desk first, so I could pretend I was asking him about a job if Drewlove came wandering by.

"Just the way he talks to you, eh. Such a *dick*."

I laughed because when it came to Sam Drewlove stories, we were allowed to laugh at each other.

"He was like, you told me you knew how to do this, and you did it all wrong. Don't act like Mister Expert when you're Mister Still Learning. I should have said, you're definitely Mister Expert, in being a wanker."

"Mister Still Learning…"

"Yeah, real funny, eh?"

Trying not to laugh, I could only hold it in a second or two. "C'mon, that's a pretty good one, Mister Still Learning! He must be on his period. Anyway, since you're all pissed off, let's get out of here for lunch, eh?"

"Hell yeah. Twelve?"

Rain had started drizzling by noon, so we headed to the Persian place on the ground floor. Even when it wasn't raining, we ended up here a lot; if you could tally up all the dollars our office had spent in this place over the years, you'd probably run out of zeros on the calculator. But it was a special favourite for Chocolate and me, and some of the other boys in the office. We weren't so particular about what we ate for lunch, unlike some people in the office, especially Angie and Korean Amy and the rest of the girls, who liked to eat Japanese one day, Chinese the next, burgers the day after, until they'd sampled five different cuisines for the week. Lunchtime was an eating ritual for them, but for us, we preferred to cut down on the commute time of walking to other corners of the city, instead spending the whole lunch hour unwinding downstairs in our Persian hideaway.

15

It was a huge place, probably thirty tables, taking up the whole of the ground floor. They even cleared it sometimes to hold community events and religious gatherings in the evenings and weekends, which we had caught the beginnings of a few times, usually while leaving the office late, or stumbling back into the car park drunk and early on Saturday and Sunday mornings. But during lunch hour it was simply Pride of Persia, our escape from timesheets and taxes and the Mister Expert upstairs.

The owner was a short, burly man with an impressive beard and soft brown eyes the colour of Maltesers. At least we presumed he was the owner; we'd never seen anyone else behind the counter. And we knew him well, and he knew us, and we always greeted each other with big smiles like old family friends, though we didn't actually know his name and he didn't know ours. He just referred to us as gentlemen. "How are you doing, gentlemen!" he'd say. And we referred to him as man. "How's it going, man?" we'd reply. And since him being man and us being gentlemen had always worked just fine, we had never thought to call each other anything different than that.

Funnily, we happened to know more about his son, from the paintings and photos he stuck on the wall by the till. We knew his son's name, from the crayon drawings of cars and horses and what I guessed might be a windmill, the words *Ashraf Hussein, Room 8* scribbled underneath or up the side, and the school portrait photos with *St Thomas Primary School* printed on the header. School and a name, and his classroom number – not much, but more than we knew about the father.

That didn't stop us from trying to know. There was one afternoon when Chocolate and I spent the entire lunch hour debating where he was from and concluded most likely Iran or Egypt or Turkey, or one of those Middle Eastern places. Then we figured if he had opened a Persian restaurant, most likely he was from a Persian country, though neither of us knew where Persia was or even what Persian people were supposed to look like. Of course, we could have solved all those riddles easily by walking ten steps to the counter and asking him, but it seemed a bit odd to do so, so we never did.

When dining at Pride of Persia, I usually took the lamb kebabs, Chocolate usually took the meatballs, but that day we swayed from the usual and both ordered the Persian fish. It was new on the menu, and I wasn't sure why it sounded so good – there was no photo of it, and it wasn't described in any particularly delicious way. But I decided I wanted it almost instantly, and it must have been quite the Jedi mind trick, as it seemed to work equally well on Chocolate too. Then, of course, we both ordered the Turkish yoghurt drink. The oddity about that drink was I didn't even like it that much, but for some reason I always ordered it, and Chocolate often did too, then while drinking it I always noted how it wasn't all that enjoyable, but I always seemed to finish it, and always ordered it again the next time.

Just as the food arrived, Chocolate pointed his eyebrows behind me. "Here's Jeffy."

As I started to turn, two hands slapped down on my shoulders.

"You two again! You two spend more time down here than you do at your desks!"

I kinked my neck up and grinned at him.

"Shucks mate, took your time," Chocolate said. "We thought you'd ditched. Another box to clear at the docks or somethin'?"

Jeffery the Scotsman was always invited to our lunches, and always late, so we never waited, especially since he often never showed up at all. He rarely missed the days we ventured out for pizza or sushi, but it was rare he joined us down at the Persian. He didn't seem to like that place much, perhaps because we ate there too often, and he only ever ordered the falafels, and I suppose a man can only eat falafels so many days in a row.

Jeffery the Scotsman worked in a team two 'blocks' down from ours. His desk was only twenty or thirty steps from mine, but in our office that was far enough that you hardly saw or heard each other, except for morning and afternoon teas, and maybe once or twice a day at the photocopy machine. Despite the nickname, Jeffery the Scotsman had not a trace of Scottish in his voice, but his father did and was proud of it. His father, named Scott, of all names, had come to New Zealand as a teen and done his school years at Hamilton High School, the same school Jeffery the Scotsman ended up at twenty years later.

We'd even had the pleasure of meeting his father once, when I'd dropped him and Chocolate home one morning after a Friday night bender. As soon as he'd seen Chocolate and me in the front seats, he'd invited us both in for breakfast, which was the last thing I had wanted at the time, but it turned out to be quite the Saturday morning around the Scotsman's breakfast table. I hadn't even known Jeffery lived with his father, but there he was cooking up a storming English breakfast when we pulled into the driveway – eggs, sausages, bacon, beans, black pudding, and I'd never had better hangover food in my life.

None of us were in any condition to be chatty that morning, but that was fine – Jeffery's father was a talker, and we learned a lot about Jeffery's father that morning – mostly that he was an army man, and a car man, and made most of his money flipping cars and fixing cars and painting cars, and that 'he'd even gone to work on a Formula 3 team, once'. Later Chocolate brought up Braveheart, as if it were the only Scottish thing he could think of in his still-drunk half-Samoan one sixteenth-Chinese brain, and Jeffery's father scoffed, calling it the worst movie ever made because they 'totally fucked up our history an' that', and 'even Harry Potter was a more Scottish movie than that fuckin' trash'.

Jeffery looked much like his father; they were both of average height and skinny, both had the same light brown eyes and sharp nose and shark-toothed grin, and the curly hair that didn't look so curly when cropped short but quickly got out of control if it grew one or two inches too long. Jeffery the Scotsman wasn't as gruff as his father – he stayed clean-shaven while his father kept a beard both short and thick, and his dad was a pinch shorter and a little more square in the face. But they looked every bit like father and son and were even more similar between the ears.

We already knew Jeffery the Scotsman was a born wheeler and dealer, and several times a week he disappeared from the office for half an hour or so, maybe even an hour in the late afternoons, or he'd take a two-hour lunch and tell his manager he was off to the dentist or had an appointment with his therapist. But we knew he was just out there picking up a car or dropping off a bunch of cellphones he had parallel imported. If we tried that nonsense with Sam Drewlove, we'd be meeting with the HR lady every week fighting for our jobs, but Jeffery worked in Peter Mack's team, and Peter Mack's reputation was he really didn't give a shit about anything. So, Jeffery juggled a bunch of mini hustles on the side of being a full-time accountant, and we were always amused at how dedicated he was to it all. "Can't make lunch, boys, picking up a car," he'd say. All for an extra two hundred or three hundred bucks a week. But after that morning, we'd learned he couldn't help it. It was in his DNA.

Jeffery ordered at the counter, with the owner whose name we didn't know, then sat down with a Coke and ripped it open.

"Jeff," I said, sipping yoghurt. "Where you think that guy's from?"

"Who?"

"The owner."

He turned around and looked. "Persia, obviously."

"Yeah, but where the hell is Persia?"

"Fuck knows. In the Middle East somewhere."

"What, like around Afghanistan up there?"

"I don't know, man, it's up there somewhere near all those Aladdin countries."

Chocolate wiped his mouth, then sipped his yoghurt. "Actually, where is Aladdin from?" he asked. "They don't tell us in the movie, do they? Kid freaking loves that film. Just watched it with him again last week."

"He's from Persia, like him," Jeffery said, nodding his head behind him.

Chocolate and I laughed and put another forkful in our mouths.

"Wherever Persia is, they know how to make fish. Might have a new winner down here."

"Yeah but, seventeen dollars for fish?" I spat out another bone and shook my head. "Good luck eating that every day on a GW salary."

"Mate." Jeffery laughed. "Chocolate's ol' ex loves his GW salary. Probably eats Persian fish twice a day."

"Yeah and feeds the kid Marmite sandwiches."

We all hooted as I stole a falafel off Jeffery's plate. Then Chocolate did the same.

"She's actually been okay lately. Kid told me she's been making him quiches for lunch. Nice ones, too."

"Time to get back together, then?"

I dropped my fork and laughed. Jeffery the Scotsman did too. But Chocolate laughed the loudest.

***

At Grant & Woodson, there were two halves to the office floor.

First, there was the West Side. That side of the office was lined with the partners' offices, with floor-to-ceiling windows, views of Victoria Park, and fancy name plaques on each door. As the tallest building on that edge of town, the view from their windows stretched over the park fields, across the market next door and all the way into the harbour. Their offices weren't lavish like something you would see on *Suits*, but they were a nice size. Big leather chairs. Lots of shelving. That sort of thing.

Right beside them were the managers' cubicles, with big L desks and big computer screens. They were each walled with high dividers – I guess to make them feel like offices without being offices. But it just meant people rarely saw or talked to each other on the West Side; in the busy season, we could go days without seeing their faces unless we actually went into their cubicles to visit them.

Down the middle of the office was a walkway that split the floor in two. That strip was like the railroad tracks separating the town into east and west, and if the west half was for the bosses, the east half was for the grunts.

That's where we lived.

The cubicles on the East Side were a quarter the size of those on the West Side, but to be fair, they still weren't tiny. If you had a file open on your desk, a glass of water, a plate with leftover morning tea on it and a keyboard and mouse, even then, as long as you kept your calculator and stapler and hole punch to the side, you still had room to slouch over and rest your head. And every grunt knew you needed to do that at least a couple of times a day.

We were crammed a little closer together on the East Side, too. But to be fair, we weren't that close together. Chocolate and I were separated by a shelf, but it only stood shoulder-high. I always liked to roll my chair around the shelf to talk to him, but I didn't need to – that shelf was low enough that if I just stood up, I could see and hear him just fine.

That was the reason, we quickly learned, why life was better on the East Side. We worked like grunts, got paid like grunts, but we had each other, and we talked, and we shared M&M's from the vending machine, and if someone warmed something up in the microwave, you could smell it drift over the tops of our cubicles. *Yo, what's that? Who's got pizza?* And on a slow day, you'd go searching and ask for a bite. That's because even between teams, everyone knew each other on the East Side. Jeffery the Scotsman was two whole blocks down, and even then you could smell his Vogel's toasting every afternoon. He ate it in the oddest way – with both Vegemite *and* Marmite, spread on one after the other. I thought he was just being funny the first time I saw it, but I didn't know him then. After a month or two, it seemed like a completely normal Jeffery the Scotsman thing to do.

Sam Drewlove's team was made up of six. On the West Side, there was Drewlove and our two managers; Brett, a tall, jolly man, also a Scot, who'd moved to New Zealand not too many years ago, and Renuga, a soft-spoken Sri Lankan woman, who was impeccably neat and never stopped giggling. I liked them both just fine; I guess because they were reasonably normal West Siders, compared to the rest of them.

On the East Side, our team had me, Chocolate, and Angie Buckle.

Angie Buckle had started in January that year as our new graduate. She was a small, dainty girl, with large spectacles and a thick, wavy ponytail that fell just below her nape. If you had to guess, you'd probably wager she was the type of girl who was a librarian at school, cut the crusts off her sandwiches, and played an instrument like the clarinet (I later found out she wasn't a librarian but did love reading, didn't cut the crusts off – just never ate them – and had never played an instrument in her life). She wasn't a shy person once she got talking, but she did have somewhat shifty eyes and a reserved demeanour that made it hard to pick her mood on any given morning.

Our friendship started just fine, but it was a work friendship, and I could see she found it hard to blend with the dynamic Chocolate and I had built in two years without her. But, slowly, as the year had gone on, she edged her way into the circle, and once or twice we offered a joke to her, and then she just began asking, 'What's so funny?' We'd sometimes tell her, sometimes not, until one day she stopped asking and started demanding, and soon she was so sisterly I couldn't spend more than two minutes at Chocolate's desk before she rolled her chair over and joined the conversation. We figured, if she was comfortable enough to do that, she was comfortable enough to get a nickname.

We started calling her Buck.

Buck asked not to be called Buck, but she only kept that up for about a day until she gave up. By that time, it had already spread through the office and when that happened, there was no going back. Even her office-best-friend Korean Amy had started using it, and Korean Amy knew as well as anyone how a nickname stuck in that office, although luckily she seemed to quite like her one.

Chocolate made it a tradition that when someone new started in Team Drewlove he took them out for dinner. He had done it with me, he'd done it with our graduate the year before, who had since left, and a few weeks after Buck started, he did it with her as well. Everyone in the team had been invited, of course, but our West Siders always had something to do with a son or a daughter, or a dinner to cook, or a dog to walk, or a wife or a husband to see, so Chocolate just started asking them at the last minute – that way it was easy for them to say no, and we could pretend to be disappointed, and nobody had to feel bad about any of it.

That dinner had been arranged for a Thursday. Buck told Chocolate her favourite food was pizza, or as she liked to say, 'interesting pizza'. She had told Korean Amy about the whole thing the day before too, who, jealous that the gesture had never been recreated in her own team, invited herself, and suggested Non Solo Pizza on Parnell Rise. Jeffery the Scotsman had agreed to come too, but had to cancel at the last minute to 'sort something out', which we never doubted with him and didn't bother to ask the details.

We'd had the bright idea of walking to Parnell that night. It wasn't a short walk, maybe forty-five minutes, but we were still in summer back then, and it was one of those gorgeous Auckland evenings, where the sun was setting but the air was still warm and humid, the faint smells of ocean salt blowing over from the harbour nearby. Even though she'd only been there some weeks, Buck already had a collection of shoes under her desk – not just one or two pairs, but eleven or twelve at least (who could guess how many more she had at home) and any time she walked anywhere for lunch she would change out of her heels and into a pair of Vans or runners. How peculiar that looked – stockings, skirt, blouse and blazer, finished with a pair of skateboarding shoes down below. But we'd soon learn Buck was hardly the type of girl to care about such things. On that night she did the same for our long walk to Parnell, changing into her black Vans, and Korean Amy, not quite as prepared with her own office shoe collection, borrowed a pair of red flats.

We walked in double file, Chocolate and I up front, Korean Amy and Buck just behind us, down the long stretch of Fanshawe Street into downtown. Auckland had an interesting city centre at the time, in that it only had a dozen or so tall buildings, and the rest weren't too tall at all. Very few parts of downtown were shrouded or devoid of sunlight, and the nearby sea breeze wasn't funnelled into towers made by rows of skyscrapers. It was pleasant to walk. Buses frequented every street, but the city had no crowded subway or tram or monorail to give an illusion of busyness. People walked slowly, faces of every colour, and even during lunch hour, streets were never crowded to the point of having to weave in and out of anyone. In fact, at the hour we walked – it had been around 7 p.m. – there weren't too many faces walking about at all. The bars did have handfuls of young Kiwis, ties loose and sleeves rolled up, sipping on Radlers and Summer Ales – the trendy beers of the time – and every Esquires coffee shop had its collection of international students, studying at tables on their lonesome with their tall cups of iced tea. But there was rarely much more happening than that. As we climbed up to and through the fields of Albert Park, we walked by endless groups of university students sitting in circles on the grass, all with books out but nobody reading. Some lay on their backs and stared at the sky, some gossiped, and some listened to a friend strumming a guitar. Familiar. That had been us, once. It looked a lot more fun than I remembered.

It'd been close to 8 p.m. when we arrived at the restaurant, though even then, the sun hadn't set, so it didn't feel late at all. Nobody ordered pizza at first. Chocolate and I shared a beer. Buck ordered a Coke. Then Korean Amy ordered mojitos for the whole table.

"We have to celebrate, guys!"

She was more excited about Buck's welcome dinner than Buck.

We learned a collection of interesting things about Buck that evening. First, she was twenty-six – old for a graduate, certainly the oldest that Grant & Woodson inducted that year. It wasn't because she was an idiot – they did a pretty good job of filtering the idiots out, mostly by way of equally idiotic tests and interviews – but because she had spent some years working as a publisher's assistant before she went to university. We found that odd, only because an accounting degree was often just a segue from accounting at high school, something you fell into, usually by eighteen-year-olds who didn't have the years or imagination to come up with anything better. Yet Buck had three years of full-time salary after high school to think about what she wanted to be, and she still chose to go to university to become an accountant. We then learned she'd only ever had one boyfriend who, of course, was 'such an asshole', and that she didn't think Sam Drewlove was too bad at all. We also learned she deemed every pizza on the menu that night far too characterless to be 'interesting'. They all seemed pretty interesting to me – Hawaiian with local mozzarella, pork sausage and egg with fresh chillies. But in Buck's world, 'interesting' pizza had to be something not seen before. She ended up ordering the duck pizza, topped with plum sauce and goat's cheese, but to her that was still only mildly interesting, as 'duck pizza isn't actually that rare', and she'd eaten it once before.

As promised, Chocolate picked up the bill that night. Even Korean Amy's share. As it turned out, it was Korean Amy that made that night meaningful for Buck because over the course of the meal, she and Korean Amy bonded, and by the end of the night, it was like they'd known each other since childhood. Chocolate and I hadn't planned on it, but we fostered their friendship that night, and I was happy for Buck. In that office, everybody needed that one friend they could call a time-out with and share a bag of Doritos, someone they could vent to about Georgina and her punchable face, someone they could invite out for a long lunch and that person would always say *yes* because they knew what it was like to be having that kind of day. Everyone who made it through those grunt years at Grant & Woodson had that person. And those who didn't never seemed to last very long at all.

Tuesday

"Bro… check this one out."

Chocolate stood up and looked over at me from his cubicle. Half a Peanut Slab was jammed in the corner of his mouth. "What's up?"

"Wife is a lawyer, right? QC. Earns two million a year. Just from lawyering." I put her tax return down, picked up the next one. "This is the husband. Earns nothing. Just some fake income from one of their holding companies. Now check out the bank statements. Xbox Live, eighteen dollars. Xbox Live, eighteen dollars. Uber Eats, forty-four dollars. Xbox Live, five dollars. Dude is living the freaking dream."

Chocolate came around to my desk, grinning. "What car does he drive?"

"No idea."

"It'll be in the family trust."

I looked at him, and my mouth dropped open as if letting out an 'Ohh!' but without making a sound. Like a kid who'd just figured out the password to his sister's computer.

"You got the file for it?" he asked, looking around my desk.

I shook my head.

"What's his name?" He didn't wait for me to answer. Just flicked to the front of the tax return. "*Joseph Alexander Finch...*" he read out, slowly, like a parent about to discipline their misbehaving child. He grabbed my mouse and clicked a few times. The client database. I used this database every day, but only for finding IRD numbers and email addresses. Chocolate seemed to know his way around it a lot better than I did. He pulled up Joseph Finch, then pointed to a section called *Related Entities*. We read them to ourselves quickly, whispering like a speed reading contest.

LJF Limited.

LJF Properties Limited.

Finch Road Limited.

The Lynda and Joseph Finch Family Trust.

As he went hunting for the trust's tax returns, I realised all the time I spent with Chocolate was spent eating, drinking, or walking somewhere so we could spend time eating or drinking. I'd never actually seen him work before. I was impressed. The way his eyes flicked, how you could see his brain ticking over. Like a detective putting clues together. Was hardly a few seconds before the family trust's accounts popped up on the screen.

"Look at that, four kids." He nodded with approval, pointing to the beneficiary list. "Let me guess... private school?" He went back to the tax return on my desk, flicked to the back. "Yep." He nodded again, tapping his finger on the page. "See these rich people man, they always make a donation to some school foundation. Gives them a tax break. Or the other way you know, you see the school fees in the current account, and you know it's for private school 'cause it's like a zillion dollars or something."

If crimes were hidden in accounting puzzles, there would be no unsolved murders. No need for police detectives. You wouldn't even need a team. You could just hire Chocolate, and he would solve everything, probably just as a hobby, all while eating Peanut Slabs and drinking Lion Reds.

Then he hit my shoulder a few times. "Here we go."

All the trust assets were listed in there, houses with addresses, even cars with number plates. It almost felt wrong to be looking at it.

"Three-million-dollar house. Remuera. One-million-dollar beach house. Coromandel. Nice. And look at this one. Mangawhai. Eight-hundred-thousand-dollar *beach cottage*." He laughed hopelessly. "Can't be happy with just beach houses, these guys. Gotta have a *beach cottage* too."

The cars were listed below. He pointed to them, and we read them out line by line.

"Mercedes Benz. B180 silver."

"Mercedes Benz. CLA white."

"Mercedes Benz. GLC white."

"Shucks man," he said, shaking his head. "All that money and no originality."

Then we read out the last one together, shouting in a whisper.

"JAGUAR! XJ black."

"Mate, we need to see what his wife looks like." He pulled up Google and searched 'Lynda Finch lawyer'. A row of headshots from law websites flicked across the screen.

"Woah," I said, leaning back in my seat.

Chocolate nodded one final time. "Dude really is living the dream."

"That coming home to you every night." I whistled. "While driving your Jag all day."

"Nah, bro." Chocolate shook his head, reaching around to his desk to grab his coffee. "That dude is not alpha enough to drive the Jaguar. I bet you it's the wife that drives the Jaguar to work, and this guy drives all those kids to private school in the Benz."

"What! No way. I bet *she* drives a different Benz to work every day to flex, and she bought him the Jaguar as a birthday present or something."

As we were debating, Buck came walking back to her desk from Drewlove's office.

"Hey Buck, Buck."

She looked over at Chocolate and me, both grinning.

"Alright," I said. "Really important question for you."

Chocolate started laughing, and Buck smiled at us like she couldn't wait.

"Let's say... you're a partner at GW, right, national partner even. You make two million dollars a year, and you have four kids."

"And you have a beach *cottage*," Chocolate sang.

"Yeah, maybe even two beach cottages. And your husband is a stay-at-home. Now, here's the important part. You've got four cars in your garage. Two little Mercedes, a big Mercedes, and a Jaguar. Which one is yours?"

"And my husband does what?"

"Nothing."

She shrugged. "Then they're all mine."

Chocolate and I cracked up, and Buck looked at us, amused. I just pointed to my screen, not wanting to explain the whole backstory.

"Anyway, morning tea?"

Chocolate looked at his watch. "Yes! Thank you, Jesus."

If there was a most important time of day at Grant & Woodson, it was 10 a.m. At that hour, the whole office had a fifteen-minute morning tea break, although it was mostly the East Side that took it. The West Side was allowed it too, of course, but were always too busy, too *in flow*, to stop work and rest for a measly fifteen minutes.

For the rest of us, 10 a.m. meant we jumped from our desks like clockwork, and you could see the parade from the East Side marching down the hallways into the lunchroom.

Morning tea was important for two reasons. First, it was where the gossip happened. If anything noteworthy happened at Grant & Woodson, morning tea was where you heard about it first. Monday morning tea was always gossip from the weekend. Friday morning tea was always guessing what gossip would be created that night. And the morning teas in between were a free-for-all of complaints about bosses, about the prices in the vending machine, about Georgina pissing everyone off again like she did last week and the week before that. More importantly, it was the one time of day the grunts were alone and could talk freely about the important things like who was wearing a stupid shirt that day, or who got in trouble with whom, or how someone saw someone look at someone funny, and now everyone needed to debate whether they were sleeping together or not. Only a few West Siders ever showed up, usually the newly promoted ones. We called them moles because they fed us the inside scoop on the managers' meetings and email threads they now got cc'd into from the higher-ups. In some ways, they were the stars of morning tea, and everyone loved having them at their tables. Though it was always just a few months before they too got swamped with work, and eventually stopped joining the 10 a.m. morning tea march like the rest of the West Side.

The second and more important part about morning tea; we got to eat. That was one way the brass at Grant & Woodson kept us grounded. They fed us.

There was an in-house chef at the office, named Margot. Every day, she cooked the partners a gourmet lunch and served it in the boardroom. We never saw that food, but Sienna at reception always cleared the table afterwards, and told us it was 'exactly the thing you'd see at a five-star restaurant.' Bottles of wine, eye fillets, dessert platters. If you peeked into Chef Margot's kitchen, which was off-limits to us grunts, you could see it looked like a five-star kitchen too, with multiple stainless steel ovens and stove tops, tall fridges with glass doors packed with fresh produce and a deep sink with one of those fancy-looking hoses for a tap. When lunchtime approached, you could smell the chickens and potatoes roasting, the fresh garlic bread being baked, the sizzle of the lamb steaks grilling on the stovetops. I suppose the partners knew how evil that was, for us to smell all that food and have nothing to eat ourselves. So at morning tea, Chef Margot's job was to cook us a little something as well.

Of course, nothing looked five-star restaurant-ish about our food – it looked more like a basket stolen from a corner bakery – but it tasted like five stars, and that's all that mattered to us. Some days it was muffins, other days it was cheese-and-ham sandwiches. If we were really lucky, she baked chocolate tarts or cheesecakes. Whatever it was, it went down a roaring treat. For those of us who rushed to work and arrived late, like me, that was our only hope of a hot breakfast. The only thing to keep us going until lunch. And most importantly, for all of us, it gave us something to look forward to in the mornings. On those tough winter days when we trudged to work in the rain, a cough or a sneeze coming on, not a hope of sunshine in the sky, something to look forward to was the most important thing in the world. I don't think the partners even realised, but morning tea was the pillar to the sanity of that office; the one thing that kept the East Side from imploding day after day.

This particular day was a good day because Chef Margot had baked bacon-and-egg pie. For most of us, eating Chef Margot's bacon-and-egg pie was a trip down nostalgia lane; usually the first time we'd eaten it since the days of bake sales at primary school. The thing about bacon-and-egg pie was, it always looked exactly the same, whether you baked it at home or bought it in a store, but everyone ate it differently. That day was no different. Chef Margot's bacon-and-egg pie looked exactly like my mother's, exactly like the bakery's down the road, exactly like the one I'd been served on a plane once, and everyone ate it in their own way – some put it on a plate, some held it in a napkin, some just ate it from their hands. Some used a knife and fork, some used only a fork, some bit straight into it, some peeled the pastry apart with their fingers and ate it bit by bit. Some sprinkled salt, pepper, or both. Some put a little tomato sauce on top, some put a lot, some put nothing at all. And of all those ways, there wasn't a wrong way to eat bacon-and-egg pie. You could look at someone eating it in whichever way, maybe the complete opposite to you, and you'd still think, 'I bet that tastes pretty darn good.'

Chocolate, Buck, and I were the first ones there. Chef Margot had barely finished putting the trays out. We plated and then snagged the corner table. Jeffery the Scotsman walked in twenty seconds later. And then just behind him, Steven Black.

Steven Black was the most handsome man in New Zealand. At least, many of the females in the office seemed to think so. Even some of the males probably did. I don't know if he was the *most* handsome man in New Zealand, but he was probably in the top three.

He had moved from an out-of-town firm into our tax department downstairs, a few months into the year. That meant technically, he wasn't an East Sider or a West Sider because downstairs there was no East Side or West Side. Down there, it was more like little subdivisions of different departments – taxation, receiverships, wealth management. Still, every department had grunts; the first and second and third years, and if you were a grunt, you were considered as much an East Sider as the rest of us.

Coming to think of it, the very first time I'd seen Steven Black was at morning tea. It was croissant day that day. The girls at our table froze when he walked in as if Jude Law had just entered the room.

"Who's the new guy?" Buck asked, nudging me.

"I think that's the new tax guy."

"What's his name?"

"No idea."

"Go and ask."

"What?"

"Go ask him! Say hi."

"Why can't you say hi?"

"I can't! You do it, you're a boy!"

In the end, nobody went and said hi to Steven Black that day, and he sat by his handsome self at a table on the opposite end of the lunchroom.

Of course, we eventually got to know him, and he sat with us the next week, and he got a little more boisterous each time, and before long morning tea wasn't quite the same if Steven Black didn't show up on any given day.

It was hard to pinpoint why everyone thought Steven Black was so handsome because he was handsome in many ways. He had clean-cropped mahogany hair, always brushed neatly to the left, and bright turquoise eyes that glinted when he smiled. A few groups of freckles clustered around his nose, which was thin and sharp and perfectly straight. He wasn't tall, wasn't short either, though he did have broad shoulders, and the shirts he wore, always with a skinny tie, fitted his athletic frame so perfectly you could almost think they were painted on.

The more interesting thing to me about Steven Black, though, was why he bothered showing up to work at all. He came from old money down south and moved to Auckland just for the job. That seemed peculiar to me, and as our friendship grew – Chocolate and I spent many a lunch hour with Steven Black, either in the lunchroom, or down at Pride of Persia, and many more hours on Friday nights getting up to mischief – and the more we learned about him, the less sense it made.

Steven Black's father was a ranching man, and the Black family had been breeding thoroughbreds for the track for more than a few generations. Over those few generations, they had bred more than a few champions, down on their little horse haven known as Wildercroft Stud.

If I had to describe the type of old riches being made at Wildercroft Stud – and it was definitely beach-cottage-level riches – it could best be done by the story Steven Black told us at Chocolate's house one evening.

We had this one stallion, beast. Pure breed. Neck like a tree trunk. All muscle. Everyone wanted a piece. The most perfect specimen you ever saw. We were charging $250,000 a pop to give our boy a stiffy and get him to bust a load inside one of your horses. We had guys wanting to bring their mares from up and down the country, even over from Aussie, just to breed with this thing, and we were turning them away. He was *already servicing four mares a day. That's a million a day, and we couldn't keep up.*

It was lucky we befriended Steven Black because even we managed to get our hands on a little of that Wildercroft Stud money. Sometimes Steven Black would send us a tip on the races – "Boys, old man's got a horse racing tomorrow – *El Quinto*. Says he's the most solid starter he's seen in fifteen years." And just because of Steven Black, we all had betting accounts before long, and we put up ten or twenty dollars just for a giggle whenever that email came through. We never had the courage to put up any more than that, even though we should have because Steven Black's old man was quite the horse whisperer, and we won something back almost every time.

When Chocolate moved out of home at eighteen, he moved from South Auckland to West Auckland – in his words, 'one of the nicer parts of town' – but when Steven Black moved to Auckland he also landed out west and didn't last a minute. "Trashy," he called it, and he'd found himself a little apartment on the North Shore barely two months later. But that was very much like Steven Black. He always had nice everything – nice shoes, nice phone, nice motorbike – much of which we knew could never have been paid for with a Grant & Woodson grunt's salary. But he somehow retained a small-town aloofness, never took himself or anyone else too seriously, and we all loved him that way. Chocolate and I were better friends with him than anyone, but you could have asked anyone at Grant & Woodson what they thought of Steven Black, and I'm sure they would have told you with sincerity he was a 'bloody good bloke', or something along those lines.

Barely two months after he was hired, the tax department hired another grunt, this time a girl. Her name was Amy.

Amy was also a small-town girl, of average height, but solidly built with thick thighs and a wide smile, which I found quite beautiful. I think all the boys did, but for some reason, nobody liked to admit it. We called her Blonde Amy, partly because she was blonde, but mostly because we needed to differentiate her from the other two Amys in the office. On the day Blonde Amy started, suddenly all the Amys in the office got new names, whether they had wanted them or not. Blonde Amy became Blonde Amy, the Amy who sat in the team beside ours became Korean Amy, and the Amy that worked in admin just became 'the other Amy', I guess because nobody ever saw her or talked about her or even knew what her job actually was.

It was lucky Blonde Amy got sat next to Steven Black because if Steven Black was the blokey guy who always drank protein shakes at lunchtime and Heineken on Fridays, Blonde Amy was the big sister who loved him and always kept him in check. They showed up at morning tea each day as if in each other's orbits, and if one showed up without the other, the first words out of our mouths were always, "Where's Steve? Where's Amy?" Nothing romantic ever happened between them, at least not that I ever heard about, but they were the right two people to be neighbours in that office. I guess the best way to put it in a word is, they 'matched'.

And that day, just like every other day, they came in one after the other. First Steven Black, then Blonde Amy. Steven Black bobbed his head as he entered, obviously happy at the sight and smell of bacon-and-egg pie. Blonde Amy, not so much; she screwed her nose up before turning to us and walking straight over. Steven Black stacked two pieces on a plate and walked over behind her.

"Should start baking these at home, eh?" he said, his mouth already full as he sat down. "Used to eat them all the time."

He almost finished the first piece in two bites. I'd already finished mine, and wanted to get a second, but I was wedged between Chocolate and Buck. I forked a chunk off Steven Black's plate instead.

"Hey, Amy," I said, putting the forkful in my mouth. "Question for you."

Everyone at the table looked at me.

"Let's say you make two million dollars a year, and you have four kids."

"Oh my god…" Buck groaned.

Chocolate laughed quietly, picking at the crumbs on his plate.

"And you live in a three-million-dollar house in Remuera."

"Don't forget the beach cottage."

"Oh yeah, you have a million-dollar beach cottage up north somewhere."

"Mangawhai."

"Yeah, Mangawhai. And your husband doesn't have a job, just stays home with your kids and plays Xbox while they're at school. Now, listen; you have four cars in the garage. Two little Mercedes, a big Mercedes, and a Jaguar. Which car do you drive?"

She looked over at Chocolate, then at Buck, then back at me, hesitating, as if it were a trick question. "And what do I do?"

"You're a lawyer."

She picked a little piece of bacon off Steven Black's plate and nibbled on it, thinking. "I'm gonna say… I'm driving the Jag."

"See!" Chocolate said, holding up a high five. Blonde Amy smiled and tapped his hand lightly.

"No way," Steven Black said, shaking his head. "Girls wouldn't even like driving a Jag. You ever driven a Jag before? It's clunky. If she's a lawyer type, she's driving the Merc. Mercs are easy to drive, like you're playing PlayStation. That's also probably why she'd have three of them. You know? It's like you look in a girl's closet, and she's got five pairs of the same shoe, just different colours. So they probably buy their cars the same way. Think about it… if you could buy three sports cars, are you going to buy three of the *same* car? That's a chick move, bro."

"That's what I'm saying!" I held out my fist, and Steven bumped it.

"Good point," said Buck, impressed.

Even Chocolate was silent, obviously rethinking his answer. I punched him lightly in the rib. He flinched and pushed me, laughing.

"Who we talking about, anyway?" Amy asked.

"Client."

"How do you know the models of all their cars?"

"It's in the trust," Chocolate and I both said in unison.

Blonde Amy looked at us for a split second, then nodded, looking upwards, obviously having the lightbulb moment I'd had twenty minutes earlier. We didn't have too many perks as Grant & Woodson accountants, but I suppose eating bacon-and-egg pie while snooping on all your rich clients was one of them.

I was still pulling apart the Finch family's life when work ended that day. You learned a lot doing taxes for rich people – but only the trivial stuff ever seemed interesting – how it cost three-thousand dollars to service a Jaguar, or how it was normal for the Finches to spend nine-hundred dollars at a restaurant on a Thursday afternoon. Once 5 p.m. rolled around, the office slowly emptied; Buck left first, as always, Chocolate not long after, and then the managers left one by one. By 7 p.m., Sam Drewlove had packed up his briefcase too and bid me goodbye.

As a third-year accountant, leaving the office wasn't so simple for me. It was our 'big year'; the year we sat our long and painful string of professional exams. The year haunted every budding accountant, and if anyone was looking particularly worn or sleepless or edging on insane, there was no need to explain. You would just say, "He's a third-year", and everyone understood. Every month that year we had a workshop to prepare for, presentations to create, exams to pass, not to mention a collection of eight folders the size of encyclopaedias we needed to read and memorise before the final six-hour exam in

October. Studying for exams at university was a drag but studying for these exams was an abomination.

While the rest of the office went home, the third-years stayed in the office and studied, sometimes buried in those pages of tax law until 8 or 9 o'clock, maybe even midnight if a big workshop was looming.

Nonetheless, we did it. And none of us could really figure out why. At any time we could have thrown those folders in the paper bin and said, "Fuck it!" and gone to work in a bank somewhere. But our pride wouldn't let us. Chocolate had passed those exams. Even Sam Drewlove had passed them. I was going to pass them too.

Steven Black was also a third-year, as was Korean Amy. The three of us congregated in the kitchen often while studying late, ordered pizza, and laughed at our collective misery. As I said, you needed your special group of people if you wanted to survive in that place.

That night, though, things were a little easier as a side mission preoccupied us for most of the night. We spent it at Chocolate's desk, sipping on Cokes stolen from the lunchroom fridge, preparing a surprise for him for the following morning. For hours we sat around his desk, creating a carefully planned spectacle that started as something small and 'just for fun' but quickly went over-the-top, as we knew it would. We always left late, but it was later than usual that night. Even some of the restaurants on the block were closing up by the time we left to make the long walks to our cars.

The one good thing about those late nights was, you always missed the traffic on the way home. Usually, it was well past 8 o'clock by the time I hit the motorway, and it was free sailing all the way. If it was quiet enough, sometimes I'd put the pedal down to 130, 140, drop the window, feel the adrenaline surge through my fingertips as the air went *woof-woof-woof* through my ears. During those moments, I could feel my pupils dilate, the electricity sizzle in my nerves, the engine so powerfully loud that my whole body vibrated with anticipation. The thing I loved most was when there was just one other car in sight, and I'd weave around it at speed like in a video game, that immense feeling of *cool* shivering through me. At any moment I knew, I was just one split second, one pothole, one stone on the windshield away from losing everything. That terrified me. But it also made me feel alive.

As I arrived home that night, I dropped my bags at the doorstep and collapsed on the couch. I stared around my apartment. The one I'd been so excited to move into after signing my GW contract. We'd celebrated here, my girlfriend, some friends. I'd hung my expensive shirts proudly in the closet. I bought an ironing board. Life had seemed so exciting then. I looked over at my desk, the French language books stacked against the wall. I hadn't opened them since the week I moved in. The yoga mat that sat rolled up underneath. The set of dumbbells I'd bought on special, that one weekend where I swore things would start to be different. All just decorations now. I kicked my pants off. Unbuttoned my shirt and peeled it off. Lay there in my socks and underwear, sipping on the water bottle on the table beside me. And that's exactly where I still was when morning arrived.

Wednesday

My morning walk to work had gotten longer over the last year. As I started arriving at the office later and later – 8:15 a.m. on my first day, 8:25 a.m. the next day, 8:30 a.m. for a few months, then 8:45 a.m., now sometimes as late as 9 o'clock – I was always parking further and further away.

If you arrived in the city before 8 a.m., you could usually find a parking spot barely five minutes' walk from the office. But if you got there at 8:15 a.m. you'd be parking up on the hill behind Victoria Park, at least a fifteen-minute walk away. By 8:30 a.m. all those spots were gone, and that's when you knew you were really going to be late.

So on this morning, I basked in the serene *calm* I felt because I, for no reason at all, had arrived earlier than I had in more than a year. It was eleven minutes past eight when I parked my car, and I grinned at the luxury of having nineteen full minutes to walk to work and still arriving on time.

When the morning was windless and dry, which it was that day, it was even a pleasant-ish walk to the office – through a couple of residential side streets, down the large hill towards Victoria Park, then across the grassy fields until you got to the corner where our beloved Grant & Woodson stood. The walk was always best just after summer, perhaps in late March or early April, when the sun still rose but the air was crisp, it cooled your face like a second shower, and each breath was like a faint wisp of menthol.

As I started the walk that day, I had a tingle of nostalgia, remembering the one time I was so early that I had stopped at one of these cafes for breakfast. I laughed at the memory; the mornings as a graduate where, since I wasn't rushing, I'd had the luxury of putting my earphones in and listening to music, strolling musingly, sending off 'good morning' texts to friends along the way.

Then as I passed the bookshop I remembered, it was always around this time, roughly 8:20, that I would see that girl with the freckles and the auburn hair, walking in the opposite direction. I recognised her every morning, almost like clockwork. We would walk past each other at that same time; right outside the bookshop, maybe a little sooner or a little later.

And then one day, she said hi to me.

Not with actual words, of course, that would have been strange, but instead, she looked up, pointed her eyes at me, lifted her eyebrows and then did that smile where it's not really a smile at all, just stretching your lips into a straight line, and somehow, we just know that person is saying hello without saying anything at all.

So I, out of instinct, did the same. And the next day we did it again, and the day after that, and suddenly it was like a tradition, when this girl with the freckles and the auburn hair walked past me near the bookshop, I would straighten my lips into the smile that wasn't really a smile, and bounce my eyebrows, and she would do the same, and then we would carry on walking.

I wondered sometimes, how it was possible that we walked past each other at the same spot at the same time every morning, but I only had to think until I was halfway across the park before I realised it was kind of obvious – she probably worked somewhere at the top of the hill, maybe in a Ponsonby gift store, and she was walking to get to work on time just like I was walking to get to work on time. It just so happened that getting to work on time for her put her at the bookshop, or near the bookshop, at around twenty minutes past eight. And me as well.

One morning, I decided not to say hi to her. I'm not sure where the idea arose, but it was as if suddenly I thought it was a bit odd to say hi to her, in this odd way, every single morning. So that day, as I neared the bookshop, I saw her in the distance, and I pretended I was messaging a friend on my phone, and I put a very focused look on my face. As we walked past each other I saw her look up at me, only barely, from the corner of my eye, but I didn't look up, I just kept typing a pretend message on my phone until we had gone past each other, and some minutes had passed. And at that moment I instantly regretted it and wished I could take it all back, that I could go back in time and give her the straight-lipped smile we gave each other every morning. I hoped she knew it wasn't personal; it was just an odd idea I'd had that morning, just a moment of stupidity that had nothing to do with her at all. Then I thought, surely such a small thing wouldn't upset her day too much, but I hadn't the faintest idea it would upset my day either, yet it had done so much more than I could have suspected.

The next morning, I found myself nervous as I approached the bookshop. I wondered if this time she might retaliate. Maybe this time it would be her turn to pretend she was messaging a fake friend on her phone and make a special effort not to say hi to me. Of course, I would understand that completely, but how awkward it would then be the day after that! Would we both have to continue typing fake messages every day, avoiding our morning hello until perhaps a long weekend, when the lapse of time would be long enough that we could forget about it all and go back to the way things were? But to my delight, she looked straight at me and did her smile, and I did mine, and everything was back to normal.

Then as months ticked on, I started coming to work later and later, and I started seeing her not at the bookshop, but a bit further up the hill, outside the large brick house with two balconies, then outside the hospice. Eventually, I arrived too late to see her at all. I didn't even remember the last time I'd seen her, and I'm certain she didn't either. Neither of us had known the last time would be the last time. It just was.

But now here I was again, walking down the hill, and it was 8:17, and I was almost at the bookshop.

Sure enough, moments later, she appeared in the distance. I recognised her walk, the way she leaned forward slightly walking uphill, heavy on each foot, and I recognised her red satchel, which always hung at her left side. As we approached each other she saw me, and I felt like she didn't recognise me right away, but she smiled, and it was a real smile this time. And as we passed each other, I heard her voice for the first time.

"Long time no see!" she said with a laugh.

I mirrored her laugh and chuckled, "Yeah, right?"

And we continued past each other just like we'd done so many times before.

That tipped off an unusually rosy morning for me. I had slept well on my couch, in my socks and underwear, had woken with the sun on my face, exchanged hellos with the auburn-haired girl for the first time in over a year, and walked out of those elevator doors seven minutes early. I hadn't felt that on top of the morning in… I couldn't remember.

"What in the…?" Sienna laughed as I walked in.

"What?"

"Bit early for you, isn't it?"

"Turning over a new leaf."

"I'm sure."

I sauntered up to our famous reception desk. That desk was a common topic of conversation in our office. Nobody could guess what obscene amount of money it had cost; the size of a small car, crafted from faux marble, shaped like the hull of a yacht, *Grant & Woodson* carved along the front in huge letters that glowed in our trademark blue and purple.

Sitting on the other side was Sienna, at a desk five times as long as mine, in front of the biggest computer screen in the entire office. She didn't need it, of course, but it looked impressive. Clients never saw our miserable cubicles on the East Side, but they saw that desk every single visit, and I suppose Sienna's ridiculously large screen was the firm's way of keeping up appearances.

We all loved Sienna. Chocolate thought she was quite the beauty, though my first impression was more girl-next-door, plain-faced, but certainly with pretty eyes and long straight brunette hair that never changed much from day to day. Barely out of high school, but confident, and laid back, we appreciated that she knew a lot of our business but minded her own, most of the time. Sometimes a girl would pop into reception to meet one of the boys for lunch, and we'd call Sienna up and ask, "Was she cute? How'd she look?" But she would just laugh innocently, or mockingly, and say she didn't quite see, and we knew what that meant and didn't bother asking a second time.

Sienna and I became rather close friends, at least by office standards, mostly because after morning teas, toilet breaks, lunches, going to the mailroom, the way back to my desk was always past reception, and of course, it was always more fun to stop and talk to Sienna rather than go back to work. We never had anything important to talk about; just what she was having for lunch, whether she tried Margot's tarts that morning, or if she watched X Factor the night before. And while she didn't spread gossip a lot, if there was something juicy about a West Sider, she'd often let me in on it. "One of Alex's clients just stormed out," she'd say, or "Paul's wife came in this morning, looking *pissed*." She was an East Sider at heart.

I hung my arms over the high edge of the desk. "I'm expecting mail."

"It's on your desk already."

"What! It's a surprise for Chocolate."

She looked up at me, baring her teeth nervously. "Woops."

"It's cool. Is he here yet?"

"Just got in."

I walked briskly to my desk. As I'd suspected, he'd been too busy at his own desk to notice the package on mine.

It was Chocolate's birthday that day. The surprise we had been preparing for him the night before was an office tradition. Steven Black, Korean Amy, and I had raided the printers for all the coloured paper, then wrapped everything on his desk like a birthday present. His stapler, hole punch, folders, mouse, keyboard, every pen, every paperclip, even his chair. He was still laughing, hands on hips, staring bewilderedly when I came around the corner.

"Happy birthday."

"You guys are fucking mental."

I grabbed the package off my desk and peeled the address label off the top. It was heavier than I expected. "One final present."

He took it from me, his eyebrows raised. He found it heavier than expected as well.

"Open it up. First one is mine, though."

He looked for his scissors, and Buck and I almost rolled on the floor at the sight of him searching his desk amongst the chaos before he found and unwrapped them. He cut the box open. I smiled as I watched him lift the top flaps.

"No shit!" He dug his hands inside.

It was two hundred Peanut Slabs, sitting loose like coins in a treasure chest.

"Thanks, man."

"First one's mine!"

He threw one at me.

"Second one's mine," Buck wailed.

He threw one at her.

Then he picked one up himself. We unwrapped them, took a bite, smiled at each other. Sometimes, it wasn't so bad, coming to work early. Not on a day like this.

Word had gotten around quickly about Chocolate's treasure chest of chocolate bars. By the end of that day, Chocolate had eaten seven Peanut Slabs. I'd had two. Buck had had two. Half the East Side had had at least one. It was a good day at Grant & Woodson.

We had planned to all go out for dinner that night, but the Auckland rain set in during the late afternoon. We never got snow during our winters, but it rained often and when it did, it bucketed. Auckland city rainstorms were loud and hit the pavement with vicious slaps you could hear all the way up on the top floor. One look out the window and you didn't even think about it. You were staying in.

The third-years were all staying after work to study anyway, so I suggested we order a few extra pizzas and they could all join our dinner in the lunchroom. Chocolate thought it was a fine idea. Korean Amy ordered our usual study group menu – a Hawaiian, a triple-cheese and a vege-supreme – multiplied by three, and Chocolate, Buck, me, Steven Black, Blonde Amy, Korean Amy, and the Scotsman all met in the lunchroom for a birthday feast. Even Sienna joined us for an hour and a slice. We didn't have a cake, so we got a few Peanut Slabs, smashed them up and Chocolate stood a lit cigarette in the middle. Then, after he made his wish, we all picked at it for dessert like a box of chocolates.

When the pizza boxes had been emptied, stacked to the side covered in grease stains, and the Peanut slabs had long been finished, Sienna said her boyfriend was downstairs and got up to leave. Buck saw that as a good opportunity to make her exit too. The rest of us sat there, sipping on Cokes from the vending machine, the third-years just procrastinating, the rest waiting for the rain to die down. I was half a mind away, down off a sugar high, now possibly in a food coma, my thoughts wandering into the odd corners it found itself going sometimes. I watched Sienna and Buck flick their coats on and wondered what they might talk about in the elevator. I wondered if the girl with the auburn hair had walked home past the bookshop yet. I wondered if Sam Drewlove was still at his desk, and whether he heard us in here and felt left out. I looked at Jeffery the Scotsman and Chocolate and Steven Black arguing about which beer was best, and wondered why they always seemed to talk about this, *every single time*.

I didn't know it at that moment, but as I sat there that day, I had already met all of the most important people of my life. These were their faces. One of them would become my best friend. One of them would become my wife. One of them would become the most famous person in the country, for a day. And one of them, with just a few words, would change my life forever.

Part 2

Ten years ago, there had been nothing here. No Grant & Woodson, no expensive bakeries, no shiny townhouses, no string of cafes lining the harbour a kilometre away. All that stood here was Victoria Park. A lone field opened in 1905, named after a queen that had died just a few years earlier. But it was so far from downtown, most didn't even consider it part of the city centre.

It stayed that way for years – just the park on its lonesome, a meaningless landmark you passed before exiting the city. Nothing of note stood within three blocks in any direction. Some may remember the lone fish market, the bruised waterfront stretch of abandoned buildings, the few wooden apartments from the sixties barely holding together. But nothing you would ever look at twice or remember. *I forgot this was even here*, many would say as they drove past.

However, even then, Victoria Park was much more than just a field lined with London plane trees. There was history in that park. Great Britain and the NZ Maori had played a rugby league match there once. During World War Two, US soldiers were housed there in temporary barracks. At the height of the 1918 flu, the fields were lined with bodies - a temporary morgue while the city figured out how to bury that many dead. Over the years, wealthy businessmen had tried to close the park, more than twice, in an attempt to build a mall or a skyscraper, or something else that would surely be worth many slabs of gold today. *The city needs a new car park, and there is no better place than here!* But they never did. Through one hundred years of wars and plagues and property sharks, the park survived.

And now, it seemed, it would survive forever. Every few years, a new building popped up, a new bakery opened. The Grant & Woodson tower was built right across the street, on the park's doorstep. It couldn't have been built closer if they'd tried. The national airline opened its regional headquarters just a block over. Old buildings got bulldozed and replaced with fancy coffee shops and boutique consulting firms. The apartments surrounding those fields were spruced up, and slowly the tenants changed from students living on toast and ramen to young professionals living on ASOS subscriptions and fancy credit cards. It was just a ten-minute walk to the harbour, where dozens of chic bars and restaurants – the kind that served Austrian craft beer and *antipasto* – opened along Jellicoe Street looking over the water. The only thing that stayed the same was the park, standing in the centre like a proud grandparent, watching the world blossom around it. The fields were always green. The trees were always tall. The feet that trod across it every morning evolved, but for a hundred years, Victoria park survived, and didn't change at all.

Thursday

I didn't know any of this back then. To me, it was always just *the park*, another section of my morning walk to work. On this particular morning (for the second day in a row, my sleep pattern had upended, and it seemed I was now coming to work early again) I decided to walk under the trees along the sidewalk, rather than across the grass, remembering how my socks had gotten wet the day before, and perhaps there was a leak in my sole I didn't know about. As I strolled along, dodging puddles from the night rain, clouds of fog exited my mouth each time I breathed, and I pretended I was smoking a cigarette like I used to do on school mornings as a kid. Just two minutes earlier, I'd said hello to the auburn-haired girl outside the bookshop. Apparently, our relationship had elevated from straight-lipped smiles to one-word greetings. She'd said, "Hey."

We passed, and smiled, and I'd said, "Hey" right back.

Afterwards, I replayed it in my head and wondered if I should have said something different. Maybe it sounded like I was copying her, and now she thought I was unoriginal. I decided the following day I would say something new, perhaps even more than one word. Something a little more adventurous like 'Good morning' or 'Have a nice day'.

When I hit the double doors of the Grant & Woodson tower, I caught Jeffery the Scotsman coming in at the same time.

"Bit early, aren't you?" He laughed.

"New leaf."

"Drewlove crackin' the stick, eh?"

We both smiled, lacking coffee, and took a silent trip up the elevator.

We didn't spend much time alone together, the Scotsman and I; he was one of those friends you seemed to only see while with others, which meant you never really got to know him *that* well. You knew things like his lunch preferences, and where he went to school, but not so much about what went on in that mind of his – things like what his aspirations were, what he was afraid of. He was always friendly, smiling, and willing to sink a beer and have a good time, but a mystery, too. The type you wouldn't be surprised by if you found out he enjoyed bird watching, ballet, death metal, or some other obscure interest that would seem bizarre for anyone else. On Friday nights, he was always the first to offer a round, always asked if you wanted anything when he ran off for food, always made sure you had a ride home, but you never saw him chatting to a lady, or dancing, or talking outside with strangers over a cigarette. He just sat there and pounded beer after beer, that distant lull on his face. Though I suppose I wasn't much different.

We didn't say anything as the elevator doors opened on the top floor. Just jutted our chins at each other as he walked off to the East Side. I went to reception to see Sienna.

"I need a card."

She held a finger up. She was on a phone call. I waited while she clicked her mouse around the screen.

"He's free all of Tuesday if that suits?"

She smiled brightly as she said it, as if the person on the other end could see her face.

As I stood waiting for her to finish, I looked down at her hand, *click-click-clicking* on the mouse. Her nails were painted bright blue, I guessed to match the blue headscarf she was wearing that day. Then my eyes flicked further down her fingers. She had a ring on each one, including her thumb, which was also blue. Further up her wrist was a Swatch watch, white face, but a custom band with blue and white stripes. I wondered how it was possible she had time every morning to organise her daily outfit down to such detail. I barely had time to match a shirt to a tie.

"No, it's not an engagement ring."

I'd been staring, obviously. Her words snapped me out of it.

"What?"

"That's always the first thing people ask when they see this one." She held her hand up, wiggled her fingers unenthusiastically. On her ring finger was a silver band fixed with a rock. "I just wear it on that finger because it fits. My grandma gave it to me."

"I didn't even… I mean, when you get engaged… I didn't even know that was the specific finger."

"Yeah! Ring finger left hand. How do you not know that?"

I shrugged. "Because I've never been engaged?"

"Weirdo." She reached down into her drawer, glancing at me like a tired older sister.

Grant & Woodson was a new building, and they had bragged to us during recruitment about how modern it was. 'Global safety standards' was the recruitment lady's catchphrase, citing how staff safety was their primary concern, and security in that building would be considered the highest quality anywhere in the world. After three days, we realised all that meant was the building was three times more annoying than it needed to be. Firstly, the toilets were in the stairwell. To get there, you had to leave the office through the fire exit opposite reception, through a steel door that looked like it belonged in a nuclear bunker. Not only that, the toilet door itself had a keypad with a special access code, which they changed every two months. Then, to get back into the office, you needed your special staff access card to open the nuclear bunker door again.

It all looked and felt very fancy, but since every staff member knew the code and every staff member had an access card, I didn't see how it made anybody safer at all. All it seemed to mean was clients kept getting locked in the stairwell, and you could hardly hear them banging through that ridiculous steel door when they did. And staff kept forgetting the access code, which meant half the times they went to the toilet, they had to come back to reception and ask Sienna before going back out again. Eventually, she just stuck the code on a Post-it note on the back of her screen, so she didn't have to spend half her day reciting the same four digits to every person who needed to take a shit.

Then, of course, people like me always asked to borrow the reception cards, which were supposed to be for visitors. We always left our access cards in our cars, at our desks, in our bags, or simply couldn't find them, and especially after lunch, nobody was going to walk all the way across the office to the East Side to get their card and then all the way back to the toilet.

Sienna pulled a card from her top drawer and handed it to me. I took it from her bright blue fingernailed hand and waved it at her with a wink.

"Last time," I lied, shoving it in my back pocket, and pushing through the steel door to the toilets.

I never liked sitting on the toilet at work, but coming to work just a few minutes earlier had seemed to upset my morning rhythm, and now instead of getting that business done at home, I felt nature calling just as I arrived at the office. From memory, I hadn't needed to perform a morning potty sit at the office since my first year.

There were only two cubicles in the male toilet, and both were free. I chose the furthest one from the door. As I stared at the seat, it looked clean, probably even cleaner than my one at home, but the idea that thirty other backsides had graced it that morning gave me pause. I unrolled three long tugs of toilet paper and wiped the seat vigorously. Unrolled three perfect strips and lined the toilet seat with them. Then unbuttoned and sat down.

Just as I did, I heard someone else walk in. As the door clicked open, I prayed their footsteps would trail over to the urinals. But they didn't. They trailed towards me, then stepped inside the cubicle beside me, followed by the unusually loud *shick-shack* of the cubicle door locking. I started praying he might be one of those strange fellows who, despite there being urinals available, had some unshakable preference to pee into a regular toilet bowl instead. But he wasn't. I listened to the clink of his belt as he dropped his trousers and sat down. I could tell he was not as hygienically predisposed as I was, as there was no delay to wipe down the toilet seat or line it with toilet paper. With him, it was bare bottom to seat without a wink.

Then we sat in silence. Just the two of us. Waist-down naked men, sitting a metre apart with our pants down, divided only by this flimsy partition, no idea of who each other was. The etiquette of how to behave was complicated. Of course, I wanted to pass my daily bowel movement as quickly and comfortably as possible. I needed to. One could even argue a healthy morning bowel movement was essential to being able to perform my duties as an accountant that day. But bowel movements come with noises and smells and sometimes, the odd whimper; all totally normal, of course, on any regular morning, but suddenly seemed unseemly with someone else so nearby. As my stomach fluttered and I felt a stool coming – normally I just let them fall at their own will – but this time I tried to ease it out, as silently as possible, and hoped for a clean splash like an Olympic diver piercing the water like a knife, not a loud one that belly-flopped and left rebound spray all over your thighs. Then I felt a little churn in my colon and did my best to engineer any collateral passing of gas to come out stealthily like a leaking tire, rather than a blubbing balloon. Finally, that first stool passed, with great relief, and though the splash wasn't great, it wasn't horrendous either; the gas had been a false alarm, and everything passed with barely a sound.

My neighbour wasn't so courteous with his morning ritual – from his side of the wall, after an uneventful opening thirty seconds, came a fast and furious, sour-smelling airstrike of continuous onslaught. Unpleasant in every way, as one would expect, though that is not what preoccupied my mind. It was now my exit I was wary of. I was cleaning myself up and was almost ready to flush, re-pant myself and go. But what was my neighbour doing? He had been silent for some seconds and hadn't moved, and I suspected he had a second round on the way, just a little roadblock in the intestine, perhaps. I was hesitant to button up and leave my cubicle because while washing my hands, the last thing I wanted was for him to also leave his cubicle, and then we'd have to see each other and navigate the interaction of saying hello while pretending not to have heard each other's intimate moments just seconds earlier. What could you even say? *"Hey, sounded like you had a healthy passing in there!"* Every time I saw that person in the office from that day, it would be the first and only thing I would think about. What if it was one of the partners? Or that oafish guy down in audit who tried to blend into your conversations at lunch sometimes? What if it was Drewlove, for heaven's sake! No, I'd much rather our identities remained a mystery. I decided to play it safe, stay in there another minute or so, and hope this person left first so we could all save face and I could wash my hands in peace. Ten seconds later, my prediction proved correct - my neighbour offered a second, but slightly milder onslaught, then without much delay, I heard the rumble of the toilet paper unrolling and sighed with relief. I was fully dressed now, ready to go, just standing in my cubicle waiting for my all-clear. My mystery neighbour wiped and reclothed in record time – couldn't have been ten seconds at most – then once again, I heard the *shick-shack* of the lock and the sound of footsteps to the sink. Water. Air dryer. Footsteps to the door. Click. Silence.

I waited an extra ten seconds just to be sure – maybe he'd return for a forgotten wallet, or access card, or pair of spectacles – and then all my manoeuvring would've been for nothing. But he didn't. I unlocked the cubicle and stepped out. Washed my hands. Took an extra minute to be doubly safe. Then walked innocently back into the office. Now I could start my morning in peace.

When I got to my desk, Chocolate was standing there with a coffee, talking to Jeffery the Scotsman.

"Drewlove's gonna come over here and whoop both your asses," I said as I saw them.

"He's not here."

"What?"

"He's in Wellington."

"Ohhh yesssssss." I raised my arms in triumph, the way I'd done as a child when I'd gotten a Nintendo for Christmas. My smile stretched from ear to ear. So did theirs.

"What's he doing down there, anyway?"

"Dunno. West side stuff. Who cares?"

"Not me." I threw my bags under the desk and went to the lunchroom to make a drink.

When I first started at Grant & Woodson, Chocolate used to offer me coffees throughout the day. We had one of those fancy coffee machines in the lunchroom; those German ones the size of a dishwasher with all the options – black, espresso, cappuccino, latte, mocha – and you just pushed a button and watched it *rrrrrr* and do its magic. So it wasn't any bother to make two cups instead of one, and he visited that machine at least three times a day. At first, I would always nod and request a mocha, but it was just to be polite. I felt bad saying no to such a kind gesture every morning and afternoon. But as we became friends, I started saying no, and then eventually I didn't have to say anything. Just a quick shake of the head, a little scrunch of the face, and he knew what that meant. It was nothing to do with him of course, or that I didn't like mochas. I just had my own drink I liked to make, and only I knew how to make it.

It started with the hot chocolate option on the coffee machine. I would drink one most days, and it was fine, but tasted flat, and sugary like cheap candy. Then one day I saw the big jar of Milo in the pantry, so I started adding a scoop of that, and that was a vast improvement. Some weeks later, I noticed there was a 'steamed milk' option on the coffee machine, almost hidden, with its own little white button in the corner. How bizarre, I thought, to hide an option that was so versatile and useful. It should have been right in the centre! So that day I skipped the hot chocolate button altogether, filled a cup with steamed milk, and added a scoop of Milo, and it was even more amazing than I'd predicted. A few days later, I decided to put two scoops of Milo instead of one, and it was so good I drank four cups that day. The next day I tried three scoops, and as impossible as it seemed, that was better still. Later that day, I tried four scoops, and that's when I realised even Milo could go too far, and three scoops was the magic number. But the final perfected recipe still needed a little touch – a generous layer of freshly sprinkled Milo over the frothing milk on top. And with that, it was perfect. I called it the Secret Milo.

Earlier in the year, we had a few summer interns join us during January. None of us could understand why, since there was never any work in January – all our clients were on holiday and the tax year didn't even finish until March. But I guess the partners were pressed to keep up appearances; big firms were supposed to have interns, after all, so they hired four or five scrappy students to dress up in suits and come to the office to read tax law all day.

One morning, an intern named James came walking around the East Side.

"Hey, morning guys."

He was a cheery lad, tall and thin, with shortly cropped red hair, and a boyish grin. Within a week, he'd been nicknamed. We called him Redhead James.

"I was just wondering if you guys had any odd jobs you wanted done? You know, anything at all."

Chocolate shook his head, but I was actually semi-busy with studying that day and called him over. "It's not really a job, but it's something to do, if you're up for it."

"Anything, man! I'll clean your shoes if you want! I been reading that blimmin' tax bible for three days now."

So I explained the Secret Milo recipe to him, in perfect detail; how the Milo had to go in first, three scoops, how he couldn't use boiling water, or fridge milk, but only steamed milk from the coffee machine. I explained where the steamed milk button was hidden and assured him while the cup might appear somewhat empty after one fill, and he might be tempted to push the button a second time, that once was more than enough – the cup would fill with froth once he stirred vigorously for ten or twenty seconds. Then I told him how the final garnish was as important as the drink itself – a fresh sprinkle of Milo on top, so it looked worthy of all that effort, like a flat white from an overpriced coffee shop. He stared at me as I explained it, his eyes glowing like a dog waiting to be thrown his brand new toy. I could tell it was the most exciting thing he'd been asked to do since he'd started.

I'll be honest – I'd doubted Redhead James, but he perfected the Secret Milo on his first try. Even Chocolate saw how delicious it looked and his mouth watered, even though I'd made one for him before and he hadn't thought all that much of it. He requested one for himself – and Redhead James was more than happy to oblige.

But it got better. The following week, Redhead James immortalised himself at Grant & Woodson. He'd been bringing Chocolate and me Secret Milos every morning and afternoon, and I remember almost feeling guilty. I thanked him profusely every time, but he insisted it was not a big deal, and in fact, probably the most fun part of his day. Each time he'd linger for a while and have a little chat with Chocolate and me before excusing himself after a few minutes, I presume to be mindful of not wearing out his welcome. We still had work to do, after all. But one afternoon as he brought our drinks, I noticed a shiftiness about him. I thought nothing of it at first, and took a sip, Chocolate sipped his, and then we looked at each other. Then we sipped it again, and we didn't quite know why we were looking at each other, but we were. And at that moment we noticed Redhead James watching us, and he finally couldn't hold it in any longer and grinned like a guilty schoolkid.

"Notice anything?" he asked nervously.

I sipped mine again. "Yeah dude, it's… different."

Chocolate nodded at me, then looked back at James. "Is this Milo?" he asked, looking up at him, sipping it one more time. "Tastes like… tiramisu."

"Made a little adjustment." He grinned proudly.

"Adjustment?"

"But I mean, you guys like it, right?"

Chocolate and I both glanced at one another with unease; it felt like a joke, but normally a practical joke would involve chilli sauce in your cup, or mustard, or vinegar. But Redhead James just smiled again like a proud chef, holding back a secret recipe.

"Alright, alright. So… I used your recipe. But then at the end, I took one of those French vanilla tea bags, and one of those cinnamon tea bags, and soaked them in there a minute or two."

Chocolate and I thought it over for a second, then laughed finally, and drank a few more gulps.

"Fuckin' not bad man," Chocolate said.

"Bloody genius." I nodded at him, impressed.

"Alright, man. I'm glad you guys like it. I'll see you later." He jumped and clapped his hands before he left, like a five-year-old girl.

From that day, word slowly got around about Redhead James and his new vanilla and cinnamon Secret Milo. It was so good, and he delivered them to our desks so promptly and without complaint, I didn't even care he was getting all the credit for my recipe. Before long, he was making it not only for Chocolate and me but for Jeffery and Steven Black and Korean Amy, and even Peter Mack, and Sienna at reception, and by the end of the month, half the team down in audit too. Seemed like harmless fun, but we knew he was finally getting too popular when the email came around reminding everyone that tea bags were 'not for taking home', and if anyone knew why all the vanilla and cinnamon tea bags were suddenly going missing to let Chef Margot know.

When the interns finished at the end of February and headed back to university, HR sent an email saying they were in the process of deciding who to offer graduate positions for the following year.

If you have any feedback on our recent summer interns we might find helpful, please let us know.

I marched straight into HR and said Redhead James had been a spectacular intern and had helped

Chocolate and me immensely, despite not even being assigned to our team.

"Anything specific?" she asked.

"Oh, so many things," I replied. "We were quiet in January, so I was studying a lot, and he helped me summarise cases for tax law. He pretty much did all our team's filing in about twenty minutes. I got him to fill out some GST returns for me. Not a single mistake. Was perfect." I thought I'd better stop there before it stopped being believable.

We found out the following month only two interns got offers. Redhead James was one of them.

Of course, he wasn't working here yet, so I was now making my own Secret Milos again, only now with his improved recipe. As I stood there dunking the tea bag, I looked at my watch.

Thursday. Two more days. Just two.

It was an easier Thursday than most. With Sam Drewlove away, the stress level on our block was always lower. We took long morning tea breaks and played music quietly at our desks. Chocolate took three times as many cigarette breaks. Of course, we still had timesheets to fill – we were charged out to clients by the hour, and we all had our quota to meet. But it was always easier to fudge that sheet when one Sam Drewlove wasn't wandering the office.

Jeffery the Scotsman and Chocolate were still standing there talking when I got back to my desk.

"Long lunch then?" Chocolate asked as I sat down.

"I'm in. What's the plan?"

"Dunno. We were thinking dumplings?"

We hadn't been down there in months.

"That's a deal! Who driving?"

Jeffery the Scotsman bounced his eyebrows. "See y'all at twelve."

Jeffery the Scotsman was early for once. When Chocolate and I exited the building, about a minute past twelve, he was sitting there grinning behind the wheel, parked right in front of the entrance, staring at us through his aviator sunglasses.

"He's early!" I laughed.

"Nah, you boys are late!"

There was only one place we ever went for dumplings, and that was Dominion Road. It was a little far for the usual lunch hour, but on a day like this, lunch was as long as we wanted it to be.

Lunch hour at Grant & Woodson was between 12 and 2 p.m. You were allowed a one-hour break, which you could take any time between then, but nobody kept tabs on you. People just assumed if you weren't at your desk, you'd gone for lunch. Except for Drewlove, of course. If he came to the East Side at 12 o'clock and saw you weren't there, he'd come back at 1 o'clock sharp, and if you still weren't there, you got one of those delightful Drewlove lectures, and he'd start watching you so closely during lunch hours it was like having his thumb jammed between your buttocks for the next three months.

On the rare days he was gone, though, lunch was a celebration. We could be gone for the whole two hours, and nobody would notice a thing.

Chocolate ran around to the front seat. I jumped in the back. U2 was playing on the stereo: *Beautiful Day*. Indeed, it was.

Jeffery the Scotsman's car was an old Nissan Sunny. It was dark forest green, and that's how I knew it was old – because I'd never seen that shade of green on any other car in the country. There were other clues too; the engine sounded like it was built a century ago, and the upholstery looked like it had been left out in the sun for a thousand summers. Despite that, he managed to keep it clean and respectable. There were no rips or stains, no Burger King wrappers scattered along the back seat. The stereo always worked. He always had a scented air freshener hanging from the rear-view mirror. A ride in Jeffery the Scotsman's forest green Sunny was never too bad at all.

That didn't mean it was a great car. More than once, on a weekend trip, or a Friday night, Jeffery the Scotsman had to jump out and pop the hood and go fiddling in there with his sad excuse for a toolkit – a few wrenches and sticks wrapped in a rag in the boot. We laughed often about the one time we'd road tripped to Hamilton in the middle of the night because Jeffery the Scotsman had sworn there was a bakery down there that would be open at 5 a.m., which had the best chicken and vegetable pie in all of New Zealand. It didn't take much to get us on board; it was a Friday, and we'd all had a river of beers, so everyone thought it was a fantastic idea. It took us almost two hours to get there, and the car putted to a stop not once but twice, as it had done many times in the past. It was pitch black outside, not a soul on the roads other than a few truckers, and Chocolate, Steven Black and I all wagered we'd be calling the AA and getting hauled back to Auckland by a tow truck. Jeffery the Scotsman called our bluff by asking, "How much?" and we each put a hundred dollars on it, and of course Jeffery the Scotsman fixed his little baby Sunny up just fine and was three hundred dollars richer by morning.

We pulled up to that bakery at 5 a.m. sharp and weren't even mad when we saw the big *CLOSED* sign on the door, which said they opened at 9 a.m., just like their website had said.

"It's wrong, I grew up there!" the Scotsman had insisted before we'd left Auckland.

We sat outside that humble bakery for three hours, passing around a bottle of Jameson, a bottle of Coke and a bag of Twisties from the gas station around the corner. That gas station had pies too, of course, but we pledged we'd come all this way to eat those famous bakery pies and would settle for nothing else. As it turned out, the owner recognised Jeffery, and kindly let us in an hour early while they were still thawing out cakes and baking their loaves for the day. When we told him we'd driven down from Auckland just for a pie, he hooted with laughter and told us the pies and coffees were on the house, as long as we promised to 'always make a pit stop' there any time we drove through town. He was a clever fellow, that bakery owner, because I never forgot the gesture, and many years later I was still stopping at that bakery for a pie and coffee any time I drove down the country and had done so at least ten times since then. Jeffery the Scotsman was right, too. To this day, I never had a better chicken and vegetable pie in my life.

None of us could figure out why Jeffery the Scotsman kept driving that Nissan Sunny all those years. He seemed to have a new car to flip every week, much nicer ones, newer ones, ones that he spent his weekends fitting with new seats and new wheels and new stereos. Surely he could have flipped his own somewhere along the way. But he seemed to love that car. It was like a challenge to keep it going year after year, breakdown after breakdown. He did clean it often and wash it often, and while the forest green panels certainly didn't look new, the car didn't look like a piece of trash either. It just drove like one.

This day was a good day for Jeffery the Scotsman's Sunny, though. We made it to the dumpling spot in one piece, and as soon as we stepped out of the car we all let out an *mmmm* at the smell of stir-fries and flaming woks and steaming broths drifting under our noses. Dominion Road was like the Chinatown of Auckland, a one-kilometre stretch of noodle houses and dim sum restaurants and tea shops that never failed to fill your stomach with happiness. There was more Chinese signage on that street than English, and you'd be forgiven for thinking you'd wandered into a little stretch of Hong Kong itself. It was actually Korean Amy who had brought us here for dumplings one Friday night, during my first year, and since then it had become the Friday night feasting spot, around 3 a.m. when we'd all sobered up, were ready to forget alcohol even existed, and just wanted to have ourselves a darn good feast.

We marched straight into our favourite joint. None of us even knew the name of it – the signage was all in Chinese – but we knew where it was, that the sign was red and that our favourite table was the round one in the corner. The Scotsman ordered a round of Tsingtao beers. Then Chocolate grabbed the menu, and we waved our hands at him, giving him the all-clear to order dumplings for the table like he always did.

Pork and cabbage. Beef and coriander. Fish with chives. Chicken and corn.

The plates came out quick and steaming. We cleaned them just as fast, as if feasting one last time before Lent, soy sauce and vinegar splashing all over our sleeves. The first beers went down like tequila shots. It was the greatest thing Korean Amy ever did, introducing us to that place. We loved it like our own grandmothers' cooking, and without her, none of us would've even known it was here.

"How much money you reckon these guys make?" I asked, picking at the last few scraps on my plate.

Jeffery the Scotsman looked around, back at the kitchen, then at the plates scattered on our table. "Quarter mil a year?"

"Profit?"

"Yeah."

"You're dreaming."

"You seen what kinda crowds they bring on a weekend? Quarter mil a year, easy."

Chocolate nodded, also looking around. "Yeah, probably close to that…"

"Quarter mil? Selling fifteen dollar plates of dumplings?"

"We do the accounts for that little Italian spot, up on Symonds. They did nearly half a mil last year."

"But Italian joints, they sell wine and fancy dinners and charge you fifteen dollars for a few shitty breadsticks. These Chinese places can't rip you off like that."

"What's a quarter mil in profit?" Chocolate shrugged, doing the numbers in his head. "Seven hundred a day? That's easy."

"Fuckin' hell man, easy? Drewlove ain't payin' us seven hundy a day! We need to get out of these suits and start a dumpling joint."

"What we gonna call it?"

"Chocolate's dumplings!"

Jeffery the Scotsman clunked his beer down on the table, laughing. "Samoan style ones. Filled with corned beef, and palusami."

"Shucks, and coconut ones for dessert!"

"We'll be millionaires!"

We all laughed and lounged back in our chairs, bellies round with satisfied grins on our faces. It was times like these I always wished the world could pause, that work didn't exist, that I could sit there all day and enjoy the post-lunch glow. I wished we could be there as friends rather than workmates, let our meals digest with laughter and banter all afternoon. Lunch conversations were always so joyful; good food, jolly company, and it felt so wrong to interrupt such beautiful moments just to return to our cubicles, of all places. But that was life.

When we'd sighed our sighs and finished our beers and paid our bill and climbed back in the car and finally turned the final corner toward the office, we'd expected Jeffery the Scotsman to pull up to the entrance and let us out before heading off to park the car. But as he approached our building, he slowed, then turned into the office car park.

"Can one of you swipe me in?"

My access card was at my desk. Luckily Chocolate's was in his pocket.

"What you doing, anyway?" he asked, handing him his card.

"Gonna park in Drewlove's spot."

Chocolate snapped his head and stared at him, aghast that he hadn't thought of it himself. "Oh, you…"

"Someone needs to park there today. Might as well be the ol' Sunny!"

We laughed as the gate rattled open and he turned his forest green clunker into the parking spot, the *Sam Drewlove – Grant & Woodson* sign plastered on the wall.

"What it's like to be a partner for a day, eh!"

As we opened the doors and stepped out, we felt it too. Walking into that building through the car park entrance, it was suddenly like we'd become the big men in the building. Hard to believe a special parking space could make you feel so important. But it did.

That night after work, after everyone had gone home and I stayed, lounged over my cubicle, my brain had almost exploded from trying to study. The beers had left me in a mild daydream, and the dumpling coma had hardly helped. It was close to 7 p.m. when I went wandering over to Korean Amy's desk. She had her earphones in and slowly pulled one out when she saw me.

"You studying IFRS?"

She nodded.

"Fun, eh?"

She laughed and pulled out her other earphone. "Only a few months left."

We both looked at the ground and sighed. I picked up the box of snacks on her desk. It was something I'd never seen before. "What are these?"

"Pepero."

I pulled one out and took a bite. "Wow. It's like a cookie. Shaped like a straw. With chocolate."

"You've never heard of Pepero?"

"Should I have?"

"It's the most popular snack in Korea."

I pulled out another one and ate it. "Pretty good."

"Take the box, please! I've been eating all day. I have heaps, anyway." She pointed to a stack of boxes under her desk.

"Woah! Strawberry flavour. And cookies and cream." I knelt down and grabbed them, studying each box like they were rare jewels I'd never seen before. "Did you buy in bulk or somethin'? You must have twenty boxes here!"

"That's nothing." She laughed and opened her bottom drawer. It was the deep drawer for keeping files in, but hers had not a single file. It was filled with junk food, all Korean, I presumed, brightly coloured wrappers with foreign writing and pictures of chocolate muffins and cream and berries and whatever else would set a five-year-old's eyes on fire.

"Shuuuuucks."

She grinned. "How else are you supposed to get through a day in this place?"

I walked over and dug my hands inside. It was never-ending. "How are you even alive?" I laughed.

"There's enough sugar in here to kill you in a week. Anyway, I gotta go. Girlfriend's waiting."

"Here, take her a gift from me." She pulled something from the drawer and threw it at me. It had some English on it. *Choco pie*. A photo of some marshmallow and cookie, covered in chocolate. Like a big Mallowpuff. I smiled at her.

"She'll love it."

My girlfriend and I usually met for dessert on Thursdays. It used to be dinner, but with me staying at the office later and later that year, I never seemed to make it on time. I think she preferred dessert anyway. So did I. Dinner always took forever.

She'd chosen a little spot in Ponsonby that day. She was already inside, waiting.

I sat down. "Hey. Brought you a gift." I put it on the table in front of her.

She smirked like it was a little magic trick. "What is it?"

"Choco Pie."

"Nice?"

"No idea. Amy gave it to me."

"Amy… that's the Asian one, right?"

"Yeah."

They'd met once before, at the office mid-year party. It had bored the life out of her, since all we did that night was talk about work. Luckily the girls took her off to dance, and the boys sat and talked rugby and decimated the dessert table. It was tame compared to usual Friday nights; nobody had wanted to drink too hard with all the West Siders around, and nobody wanted to go around meeting partners' husbands and wives either. Luckily it had ended before midnight, and we salvaged the evening with some late-night drinks down on The Viaduct. That was the first and last time she met any of my work friends. Didn't mean she didn't know about them, though. In fact, it was all we ever talked about. My friends at work. Her friends at work. The lady in admin who was annoying me. The new person at her office who everybody liked.

As we picked at the cheesecake she ordered, she told me about the big 'scandal' at her job, where one of the managers was leaving, and taking more than ten staff with her.

"Such a shitty thing to do," she said, "But I bet she's getting paid something crazy."

I spooned off another piece of cake. "I bet," I said, doing my best to look interested.

It hadn't always been this way. In our earlier years, things had been quite exciting. We talked about doing a gap year in Spain, where we'd learn to dance and take weekend trips to Portugal. We said we'd save for a year, then we'd go. But then her mum had an operation, and she wanted to be around for that, then she got promoted, and then my third year began, and our talks changed to how we were a little older now, and she wanted to think about buying a house. And you couldn't spend a year in Spain when you had a mortgage, of course. A year in San Francisco would have been cool. We had talked one night about going there too, after Spain, riding those trams, watching the 49ers play, holidaying around California. We'd still be young, right? What's an extra year abroad? But she seemed to laugh at them now. "Dreams we had when we were kids," she called them. Yeah. I guess she was right. Now she liked to talk about our careers, how we were both earning decent money now, how the housing market was hot, and we really needed to start looking. "We could be homeowners in our twenties!" she'd say excitedly. "What a dream that would be, right?"

It was stale. Not just the cheesecake, but the conversation, the smiles on our faces. I wondered if things felt stale because work was stale, and that staleness made everything in life seem stale. Mornings were stale. Evenings were stale. Weekends were for sleeping. And stale. I shrugged it off. Maybe it would get better. Maybe once I passed these exams, I'd be less stressed, and life wouldn't be so *tired* all the time.

Maybe we wouldn't be stale forever. Maybe we'd still get to Spain after all.

We kissed each other goodbye and drove home. I asked if she wanted to stay the night, but she said she had early meetings. She hadn't stayed over in a few weeks, but I didn't mind, to be honest. I'd only asked because I always did and didn't want her to think something was wrong. Besides, she talked a lot when she stayed over, and I had too much on my mind these days. *The Clairewell job is going over budget. Hintons are coming in for a meeting tomorrow. Did I include the interest on that return? Why couldn't I reconcile that report today?*

For the third night in a row, I fell asleep on the couch. A bottle of water in my hand. In my socks and underwear.

Friday

"What you want?" I already knew it would be Fanta or L&P.

"L&P."

I walked into the lunchroom, where some of the boys had already settled in the corner with a round of beers. Rugby was on the TV.

"Ehhhhhh there he is. Drewlove letting you clock off early eh boy! C'mon, we already got one for ya."

Steven Black tapped a freshly opened beer on the table.

I smiled and pulled two L&P's from the fridge. "I'll be back."

I headed back to the reception desk and handed one to Sienna, and we cranked them open at the same time.

Friday night drinks were sacred at Grant & Woodson, and one of the few things they did well at that office. Each Friday morning, the fridge was stocked with classic beers, soft drinks, pretzels and potato chips, and the pantry was lined with bottles of red wine. Once 5 o'clock arrived and the week officially ended, the lunchroom filled and quickly became intoxicated, the clanging of bottles and chatter echoing all the way into the hallways at the end of the floor.

Some of the partners were regulars there too, chin-wagging and making sure they stayed friendly with the staff, and the ladder climbers were always sure to chin-wag back and make sure they stayed friendly with the partners. Even Drewlove made an appearance now and then. But slowly, around six, the partners headed back to their offices to work and later headed home. The managers went home to their kids and wives and husbands, and by 6:30 p.m., surely

7 p.m. at the latest, it was just the usual Friday crew left.

Steven Black liked to call us the rat-pack. "Where's the rat-pack heading tonight boys?" he'd ask. And once the clock hit 9 or 10 p.m. it was time to head down to Pride of Persia for a kebab or a few samosas before moving on to the bars. Sometimes we walked down the road to the wild and sprawling Sales Street Bar, other nights we hopped the fancier bars on the waterfront, but wherever we went it was always the big highlight of our week – maybe the only highlight of our week – so we never failed to spend a lot of money or have a good time. We didn't always see each other much during the week, sometimes not at all; a lot of the rat-pack worked downstairs, or were out at clients, sometimes too busy to even make it to morning tea, but we always saw them on Friday night, and sometimes didn't say bye until Saturday morning, maybe even Saturday afternoon, or on a few rare and legendary occasions, Sunday evening.

Sienna never joined us though. While we all clocked out at 5 p.m., she had to sit at reception for an extra hour, just in case someone called, or a client came in. So I always started my Friday night drinks with her, standing over the front desk, sharing a drink and a bowl of pretzels.

"What is this?" I asked, picking up the book underneath her purse. I looked over the cover a couple of times. *"A Streetcar Named Desire..."* I read out slowly. "Cool... you read this kind of stuff?"

"I'm studying it."

"You're in school?"

"University, yes."

"Since when?"

"A few weeks ago."

I smiled at her, proudly for some reason, and she smiled back.

"Well, what are you studying?"

"Drama."

"Drama? That's a subject?"

"Yes, dick. It's a subject."

"At university?"

"At university."

"So what, it's... bachelor of drama?"

"Bachelor of arts."

"Oh and let me guess... majoring in drama."

"Yes."

"See, I'm arty. So what does that mean, you going to be an actress or somethin'?"

She sipped her drink, shaking her head at me.

"Director?"

She shook her head again.

"Mmm. Screenwriter?"

"Close."

I squinted, biting half a pretzel, trying to read the hidden smile on her face. "Close to a screenwriter…" I looked at the book again. "A screenwriter editor?"

She laughed. "No weirdo. This is a play," she said, pulling the book from my hands and waving it. "A Streetcar Named Desire. A playwright. I want to write plays." She handed the book back to me.

"A playwriter…"

"Playwright."

"Sorry. Playwright. That's…" I looked at the cover again. *A Streetcar Named Desire. Tennessee Williams.* "That's really cool, actually."

She studied my face for a split second and saw I was being genuine. At least I hoped that's what she saw, because I was.

"What made you wanna do that?" I flicked through it, not slow enough to read anything, but still looking at the pages as if I could. She was silent, so I looked up at her. She was thinking.

"I saw a play once, and I loved it. And just decided… I wanted to do that."

I spun the book between my fingers, intrigued. Actually, it took me a second to realise, but I was more than intrigued. I was jealous. And I wasn't sure why I was jealous, it just suddenly seemed so… I mean… we all came to this office every day in pressed suits and worked to strict deadlines and had millionaires coming in the door to ask us for advice, and we had all studied and worked so hard for that privilege; it just didn't seem fair that the most interesting person in the building might be the girl at reception. All those years at university suffering through case studies from Harvard Business School – "We're very privileged to have access to this," I remembered them saying – and reading the manuals on accounting software, writing essays on *The Taxation of Trusts* because that's what you do at university, right? You force yourself to learn these things so you can get a job later and earn some money. And I just never realised until then, there was a whole other side of studying, where people went to university and studied things just because they liked them.

"So what do you do in a playwriting class?"

"We learn stuff like… how to create scenes, how to create different emotions, stuff like that."

"Oh. Damn."

I had barely touched my L&P. She looked like she'd almost finished hers.

"So you're going to write a play, huh? And become famous. And I can tell everyone I used to know you."

"When I was a starving receptionist."

"And I was a starving accountant."

"You're not starving!"

"I'm spiritually starving."

We laughed.

"So, how does a playwright become famous? Are there any famous ones? I don't think I know any."

"Shakespeare."

"Oh! Right."

"Oscar Wilde."

"Hey, I know him too."

"Really? What did he write?"

I shrugged. "I dunno, but he has that famous quote about following your dreams and stuff."

"Victor Hugo."

"Never heard of him."

"Hunchback of Notre Dame? Les Mis?"

"Ohhhh! Yeah. Famous for writing plays… how about that… "

For the next half hour I turned through the book, read out random scenes, asked her questions that probably sounded moronic – "Who decides how loud the music is in this scene?" – little did she know they were more sincere than any accounting question I'd ever asked anyone in that office. For once, I actually wanted to know the answer.

Once the pretzels were finished, I picked up the bowl and asked if she wanted a refill. She didn't.

"Alright, I'm gonna go see the boys. You gonna join us after?"

But I already knew what she was going to say. Not this time.

"Not this time."

And her boyfriend will be here soon.

"My boyfriend's on his way."

I handed her book back. "Alright, Tennessee Williams. Thanks for the chat."

"Thanks for the drink."

As I walked away, I held my fist up and punched the sky. And somehow, we both knew that meant "You're welcome."

That night, after all the managers had gone home, the rugby game on TV had finished, the sun had gone down and we'd been through eight bags of pretzels, Jeffery the Scotsman decided that night was finally going to be the night.

"We're going to empty that fridge."

Every Friday night since I'd started working at Grant & Woodson, Chocolate and Jeffery the Scotsman had joked about finishing every beer in that fridge. But this night, the Scotsman seemed serious. He'd even gone and calculated it – there were seven rows left of Heinekens, eight bottles in each row, six boxes of Lion Red, six cans in each one, six boxes of Amstel Lights, four bottles in each one, and that added up to only 116 beers. Between the eight guys in the rat-pack, that meant 'only fourteen and a half beers each'.

He opened the fridge again and counted a second time. "This is it, man!" he said as if looking at some treasure map, about to undertake a voyage that was going to change his life. "The clients we had in here tonight made a pretty big dent for us. We could do it tonight, seriously!"

I looked at Chocolate. He'd already had five or six, and it would be tough for him to do another fourteen (although at his barbecue a few months earlier, he had finished a dozen himself pretty comfortably). Steven Black still looked sober, and I could see he was game. Me – I'd never drank fourteen beers in one night in my life. And they knew I couldn't, too. That didn't stop them from trying.

Jeffery brought over a round of fresh Heinekens and popped them open. "Fourteen more rounds, boys. Tonight's the night."

Steven Black grinned. "Cheers."

We all clinked bottles.

And for the next few hours, as we sat there destroying our livers, and fresh bottles continued getting plonked in front of me, the laughter and shouting faded, and I drifted into a daydream. I thought about my girlfriend, at first, what she might be doing at that time, and that I should probably message her. Then I had this odd image in my head of her on a cloud in front of me, drifting away. Once she disappeared, Sienna appeared behind me, holding a box. I turned around, and I couldn't see her face, but I knew it was her, somehow. I opened the box, and a newspaper was inside. The title at the top said *LIFE*. There was a red stain in the corner, which I guessed was tomato sauce, or maybe jam from a jelly donut. Then Chocolate appeared. He had boxing gloves on, and suddenly he and Steven Black were sparring each other and laughing. Jeffery the Scotsman watched, confused. Then Sam Drewlove drove his car straight into the lunchroom. Walked right over to me and handed me a beer. I tried to drink it, but it kept spilling on my chin, my shirt, and my hands. Then I could feel the wetness running down my sleeve, and it was real, the whole thing was real. And then laughter. Just lots and lots of laughter.

"And he's awake!"

The laughter was Steven Black's. And Chocolate's. And Jeffery's.

"Relax, mate, just a little water."

I sat up quickly, smelled the patches on my shirt. Water.

"Steve's idea." Chocolate grinned, still holding the glass.

"Bro don't even try to…" Steven Black laughed.

"You been out for a minute, mate. Shucks."

"Yeah, wow. What time is it?"

"Almost midnight."

I looked around, making sure I was where I thought I was. They must have sensed my haziness.

"You orright, man?"

I rubbed my eyes. I'd slept so deep, there were crusts in the corners. "Yeah, man. I had this dream. It was like… high definition. Surround sound. Fucking IMAX or something."

"Any cute girls?" Chocolate joked.

I looked up at him and nodded.

"Yeah. Your mum."

"This guy!"

He put the glass of water down in front of me.

"Alright, mate. Slug some water. Big night tonight!"

I took a gulp, then popped a pretzel in my mouth from the packet on the seat next to me. "You guys empty the fridge?"

"Mate, you still got six beers left, then we're good!" Steven Black said.

Jeffery the Scotsman was sitting on the bench by the fridge, eating a kebab from downstairs. "Nah," he said, sounding disappointed. "We didn't. But we came close. Twenty-two left."

Chocolate turned and stared at the fridge for a moment. He could barely stand straight. "You know what? We're gonna fucking do it."

He marched out of the room. A minute later, he came back with a storage box from the mailroom. He started with the cans, stacking them along the bottom. Then he started laying the bottles on top.

Steven Black and I looked at each other, confused, then smiled cautiously. Jeffery the Scotsman sat there, still eating, watching, like it was the most normal thing in the world. "How you gonna get that downstairs without the elevator camera seeing you?"

Chocolate looked up at him, breathing heavily like he was in the middle of an aerobics session. It looked like he might even be sweating. "I'll go down the stairs."

"Seven floors?" I said.

He said nothing.

"It'll sober him up, at least," I said quietly.

"It ain't like we stealing 'em!" he shouted finally, his head still in the fridge.

"That's exactly what you're doing," I said, laughing.

He pulled the last few bottles out and set them on the bench. "Looky 'ere. We gon' drink 'em. Right? We drink 'em here, or we drink 'em down 'ere. What's the diff'ence?"

He packed the last few bottles in the box, then turned and looked at the fridge proudly.

I had to admit. It did look kind of… neat. All the top shelves were empty, and for the first time, all we could see were the white panels in the back. There were still Coke and Sprite and L&P cans on the shelves below, but we weren't looking down there. Chocolate took out his phone and snapped a photo. "That's what it looks like boys. Victory."

Steven, Jeffery and I took the elevator down. Chocolate took the stairs, with his overflowing box of stolen drinks and dropped them in the boot of his car, which he'd moved into Sam Drewlove's spot after everyone had left for the day.

By then, it was just the four of us. The rest of the rat-pack had filtered out and made their way home, while I'd been asleep, dreaming in 4K. But I was awake now. With a few pretzels and some water, I felt re-energised. Somehow ready for whatever craziness might be ahead. After all, Friday only came once a week.

As it turned out, Chocolate raiding the fridge was as crazy as it got that night. We went to Sales Street Bar and drank a few rounds, but it was quiet, the rain dampening the usual Friday night festivities. Around 3 a.m. our stomachs grumbled, and we left to get food at one of our favourite burger joints downtown.

Jeffery the Scotsman wasn't interested and decided to head home early.

After our bellies filled and our minds cleared, we made the slow and long walk back to the office. Chocolate's phone beeped.

"Shit."

"What?"

"It's Jeff. He said don't drive yet. Cops are out breath testing everywhere."

We all stopped walking and looked at each other.

"I'm sober," Steven said.

I nodded. "I am too. But the breath test won't say that. Gotta wait a few hours, at least."

It was still drizzling with rain, though it wasn't bothering us; it was light enough that the droplets just sat like weightless sparkles on our hair, rather than matting it to our foreheads. Just slightly, you could feel the air warming, the faintest glow of a sunrise in the distance.

"We got a shitload of beers, I guess." Chocolate shrugged.

Steven and I flicked our eyes at one another, smiles stretching across our faces. We'd forgotten about that. Maybe Chocolate's idea hadn't been so stupid after all.

***

We sat in Chocolate's car, in front of the water, looking out over the quiet end of the city harbour. After sitting in the office car park for an hour, we'd gotten antsy, and Chocolate had the bright idea to drive out here. Besides, it was only a five-minute drive away. And a view worth ten times as much. It was almost 7 a.m.; the sun had half-risen and the rain had gone. With a bit of imagination, it almost looked like summer.

"Fuck, marry, kill," Chocolate said, staring out the windscreen.

"Okay, who?"

"Blonde Amy. Korean Amy. Sienna."

I laughed. "Dude, that's easy." I was laying along the backseat, my feet resting on the window rib. Steven Black sat beside Chocolate up front.

"Go'n then."

"Well, I'm killing Blonde Amy."

"Definitely." Steven Black laughed. "And I'll marry Sienna."

"Eh!" Chocolate scoffed.

"What's wrong with Sienna?"

"Nothing, but she's a receptionist."

"So what?"

"I always thought, since they're both not bad looking, you just marry the richer one."

Steven Black and I thought about it.

"Nah," I said. "I'm with Stevey. Marrying Sienna."

"Shucks… you guys better be rich."

"Dude, have you seen how Korean Amy literally never stops talking, ever? You want to go home to that every day?"

"If she makin' six figures, ain't no thing." He sipped his beer quickly as if he couldn't start another sentence without another mouthful. "Once you pop a few kids, you barely god time to talk wid her anyway. At least dat mortgage'll be gone quick smart. We'll be like that couple. What's da one?" He clicked his fingers at me.

"The Finches."

"Yeah, dat guy and dat Jaguar. If you marry Sienna, it's a Toyota Corolla for the rest of your life, mate, shucks."

We all laughed. Once he had enough drinks in him, Chocolate was always the cynic – the cynic who slurred with passion and broken syllables.

"Alright alright, how about this one?" he continued. "Korean Amy. Sienna. Buck."

"Oooh." Steven Black sucked air between his teeth, thinking intensely.

111

"That's a tougher one," I said, staring at the ceiling, thinking even harder than Steven.

"I'm still marrying Sienna," he said finally.

I rolled my eyes at the back of his seat. "Of course! Wasn't that obvious? I was trying to decide who to kill."

Chocolate screwed his face up. "You guys, man!"

"What, you think I'd marry Buck instead of Sienna? Dude?" I kicked the back of Chocolate's seat like he needed a shaking. "Girl can't even eat a normal pizza."

"Yeah, she's bit of a wobbly one," Steven Black said. "So you're killing who, then?"

I shrugged. "It's gotta be Buck. I'll be honest, one night with Amy? Wouldn't be so bad."

Chocolate laughed. "Well, I wouldn't mind a night wid Buck either. She's probably inna some freaky shit."

I nudged the back of his seat again. "Yeah, she'll dress you up in goat cheese and plum sauce and turn you into an interesting pizza." I kicked the roof laughing. Steven Black laughed so hard he almost fell out onto the concrete. Chocolate was unfazed, shouting over the top of us.

"Y'all two just loving on Sienna too much. While I marry my freaky pizza girl. Jealous, eh!" He sat up, pulled another beer from the box and threw it at me.

Handed one to Steven Black. Opened one for himself. I watched him gulp it down. I guessed Chocolate had forgotten we were supposed to be sobering up so we could drive home. Or perhaps he thought the faster he drank, the faster we'd run out of beers, and then he could sober up for real.

I didn't open mine. Just spun it between my palms, round and round. Then I sat up. Opened the door. Put my feet on the ground, looked out over the water.

"You guys ever think about moving on from this?"

The sky was light now. Some were even out for their Saturday morning jogs. I didn't look at the time, but it was certainly no longer Friday night. The city had woken up.

"From what? Drinking?"

"Nah, man. Not drinking. From this. From GW. This whole thing right here." I waved my arm out at the city like a magician, as if making it magically appear for the first time. "Look at it. This city. This life."

Chocolate suddenly sobered. He shuffled up in his seat, stared out at the city with me. Like he'd been waiting for this conversation all night. "You know what, man? I been thinking about that a lot too lately."

"Really?"

"Yeah, I looked at my payslip the other day. And it's like, the taxman takes half my check. My student loan takes the other half of my check. My ex takes the third half of my check. Kiwisaver takes the fourth half of my check. And I barely got enough for a sausage roll after they give me the rest. It's like, shucks man, what the heck am I even doing here? Just paying for everyone else's life." He crushed his beer can on the dashboard and dropped it down at his feet. It almost made me uncomfortable, how serious he was all of a sudden. "That's a good idea, man." He turned and looked at me. "I should just get out of here. You know. For a few years."

"And do what?" Steven Black said. He was suddenly serious too.

"Anything, man. I ain't chasin' one o' dem West Side manager cubicles, man. There's no point me being here anymore. Shucks. I was looking at jobs the other day. They need accountants in Japan, in Italy, in New York. There's a world out there, man. I mean Italy, how cool would that be? You can eat pasta there right off the damn trees. How about that, eh? Chocolate from Manurewa, taking over the world."

"That's what I'm saying, bro!" I punched the back of his seat one more time. "I'm with you, bro. Let me shove one right up this fucking exam. And then I'm right there with you."

"I dunno, you guys," Steven Black mumbled, tipping his beer to his mouth. "It's all greener grass, I say. Look around, man. This is the best country in the world. Fuckin' Aotearoa."

"That's 'cause your dad owns half this damn country."

Steven Black rolled his eyes like he'd heard this before. Because he had heard this before.

"Probably rides one of those horses right up into parliament. Everyone bows down, hey hey hey! Mr Black is here!"

"Fuck off, bro."

"He's right, bro. It's different for someone like me," Chocolate said, grabbing another can. But he didn't open it right away this time. Just rested his hand on top while he talked. "I'll tell you what I know, man. All that shit I went through, with my mum, and my kid, and my ex. Man, I'm already a fucking miracle, is what my family thinks. Where I come from, you gotta be brave to have a dream. Nobody's ever going to believe in it except for you. You'll sound like a flippin' egg talking about Italy around there. But when you make it, they all come running. But then…" He paused for a moment. Smirked. "If you screw everything up. Nobody's gonna come save you."

Steven Black didn't say anything. I just smiled.

"Next year, Chocolate. Me and you. We're out of this place. I'm serious, man. Let's swear it."

He opened his beer and held it out. I opened mine and knocked it with his.

"Fuckin' cheers to that."

Saturday

It was around 10 a.m. when we decided to head back to the office. Miraculously, Chocolate made the five-minute drive in one piece. He parked in Drewlove's spot again. None of us had managed to sober up. In fact, in the hours we'd been sitting out there by the water, we'd gotten drunker. We all had at least a few hours before we could drive.

"Let's wait upstairs," I said. "You guys go up. I'll grab us some breakfast."

I headed to the French bakery around the corner. On the way there, I noticed the huge crowd inside Pride of Persia. A hundred people, at least. Everyone wore long beautiful gowns and those Muslim hats on their heads. Maybe some kind of prayer meeting, I guessed. I caught sight of the owner, whose name we didn't know, talking to a few men in the corner. They all laughed like he had just told a great joke. I kept my eye on him as I walked by, in case he saw me out the window and I could wave. But he didn't. The bakery was quiet when I got there. An old lady was at the counter, buying half a dozen baguettes. A few kids dressed in soccer uniforms were pointing at the chocolate tarts and looking longingly at their mother. She got in line and ordered herself a coffee. And then the tarts. I got to the counter and bought a dozen croissants. In true French style, the girl packed them neatly in a box for me, all facing the same way. They weren't cheap, but they looked delicious. And after the night we'd had, delicious was certainly more important than cheap.

When the elevator doors opened, I found Sienna sitting at reception. She laughed at the sight of me, and I wasn't sure if it was at the confused look on my face, or the tragic hair and grimy shirt and sullen face from a long and unsavoury night. But then I realised I didn't really care why. Just the laugh was enough to make me smile.

"Isn't it… Saturday?" I asked.

"It is."

"So…"

"I came to study."

"Ahhh, yes. Sienna's a student now."

"You smell like beer."

I lifted my arm and sniffed it. "Yes I do." I opened the box of croissants. "Breakfast?"

"Wow! Yes please."

Even I said wow in my head. They looked more delicious inside than I'd remembered. Ham and brie. Cream cheese. Butter and jam. Dark chocolate. As I watched her hand linger, I already knew she'd be taking a chocolate one. But she didn't. She reached in, bit her lip, and carefully pulled out a butter and jam.

"Interesting choice."

She grinned as she bit into it.

"I'll be back. I'm gon' take these to the boys."

Steven Black and Chocolate were sitting in the lunchroom, in the same spot they'd been sitting twelve hours earlier. The news was on the TV.

I pulled up a seat, put the box of croissants down and took a chocolate one for myself. "Breakfast."

"Ohhh, you flippin' legend!"

They both grabbed one, then a few seconds later, another, and as we ran through them hungrily, we pointed at the empty fridge and giggled nervously.

"Might get in trouble for that."

"Why? We drank 'em. That's what they're there for."

Was hard to argue with that.

The rugby highlights came on the screen, and we all groaned with approval, our feet up, our mouths filled with half-eaten croissants, lazy smiles on our faces. It wasn't the perfect start to a Saturday morning; each of us would have much rather been lying in our beds, well-rested, hangover-free, starting our day with a hot shower and a fresh pair of underwear. But as we were about to find out, such things would be the least of our worries that day.

In a few seconds, it would begin, and our lives would never be the same again.

Part 3

It didn't alarm us at first. I guess because we didn't know what it was.

I just looked at Chocolate, who looked at Steven Black, and Steven Black didn't look at anyone, just paused halfway through a bite of his croissant. It was silent for a moment. Then we just looked back at the TV.

Seconds later, it came again.

Bap bap bap bap!

We heard a scream. Then another.

Then that noise again.

Bap bap! Bap bap bap!

And then came a different type of scream. Not just one. Many. We froze as the sound pierced the windows and shilled through our bones, and suddenly, we weren't so asleep anymore. Our eyes were wide open. Because it was the type of scream where we didn't even need to ask. We already knew.

I bounced off my seat and bounded into reception. The boys scrambled behind me. I found Sienna crouching at the window in the waiting area, her hands pressed up against the glass.

"The fuck is happening?" I gasped, rushing over and crouching next to her.

People were running in all directions. Screams. More and more screams. Then that noise again. Louder this time.

Bap bap bap bap!

Bap bap!

Sienna didn't say anything. Just stayed eerily still, her knees pulled close together like she was huddling outside on a cold winter morning. Her cheeks were still dry, but in the cup of her eyelid, tears had started to well. She looked at me, her face white like marble. "He had a gun."

Steven Black and Chocolate stood a few metres over from us, staring at the road below. None of us knew where to look. Everywhere there was someone running, someone pointing. That noise again.

Bap bap! Bap bap!

"I know that sound," Steven Black said under his breath, his eyes unmoved from the scene below. "Gunshots."

Finally, I stood and took a few steps back. I could hear my heartbeat thumping against my rib cage, but to my surprise, my mind was crisp and unclouded. "What do we do?" I said, looking at them.

None of them moved.

"Hey!"

Finally, Sienna turned and looked up at me. Chocolate stepped back from the window and turned to me as well. His eyes threw me for a second. I'd never seen him scared before. But neither of them said anything.

"Call the police, right?" I pulled out my phone. "That's what we do. We call the police. Yeah?" I didn't wait for them to answer. *1-1-1*. It was strange seeing those digits on the screen. I'd never dialled them in my life.

"Yes hi, I… I'm calling from the Grant & Woodson Tower opposite Vic Park, I just…"

"Yes sir, we're aware and units are on the way. Please get as far away as you can, do not stay there…"

"No, you don't understand. I'm calling from inside the building. I'm on the seventh floor."

"You're *inside* the Grant & Woodson tower?"

"Yes, me and some others."

"How many?"

"Four of us."

Then, behind me, one of the meeting room doors opened. Darsh came walking out. He already looked spooked, but when he saw our faces, the frightfulness in his eyes turned worse than Chocolate's. He walked over to the window and took a look for himself.

"Make that five."

"Okay, five of you. Are you sure there's nobody else?"

I glanced back to the hallway toward the offices, where I could barely see the West Side. "No. I'm not."

She paused for a tick, as if writing something down. "Okay sir, I'm going to keep you on the line. What you need to do is get yourselves to a safe place. But make sure to stay on that floor. Do not get in the lift or take the stairs down. It's not safe. Do you understand that? That's very important to stay where you are."

"Yeah. I got it."

"Okay, secure yourselves in a room, please. I'm going to stay on the line with you while you do."

I held the phone to my chest. They'd all been watching me like anxious children. "She says we need to move to a room and stay there. What do you think? Boardroom?"

"Lunchroom," Chocolate said quickly.

"Fuck that!" Steven Black snapped. "Let's elevator down to the car park. We'll be safer there. At least we'll be on the ground!"

"No way, man, they're shooting down there!"

"Nobody can get in though, right? You need a card? We could get out the back entrance or something. Otherwise, we'll be stuck in here!"

"She said we can't!"

"Who?"

"The fucking police lady!" I waved the phone at him, surprised at the way I'd snapped.

"Man..." He shook his head, staring back out the window again. "Motherf... okay, let's go."

We hurried into the lunchroom, all trailing behind Chocolate. Sienna was crying. Steven Black was angry. Darsh was blank-faced, but certainly not smiling. I shut the door behind us and put the phone back to my ear.

"Okay. We're here?"

"Okay, good. Good. You're doing great. Now, can you explain to me where this room is?"

In painful detail, I described the path to the lunchroom, the same path I'd walked so many mornings over the past three years. First, coming out of the elevator. Then right, into the hallway. Past the first meeting room, where we'd spent the first two weeks of our careers in training as graduates. Past the second meeting room, which nobody ever used because it still had the old chairs and tables that nobody liked. Past the IT office. All the way to the end, into the lunchroom, where we spent every morning gossiping and every Friday night sinking our weekly sorrows in beer.

"Okay, I'm going to put you through to an officer who wants to talk with you, alright?"

The changeover was instant.

"This is Superintendent Delowe. How you doing, son?"

"Well, you can tell me what's going on."

He cleared his throat quickly and swallowed. "There's a shooting at the restaurant on the first floor of your building. We don't know much yet, but the building is being surrounded as we speak. I can tell you the safest thing you and your companions can do right now is stay put. The security system in your building is top-notch. We've already shut down the elevators and locked the access card system. We're turning off the power now too. Nobody can get to where you are via the lift or the stairs. Now, the first thing I need to ask of you is to stay away from any windows. We can't have any media seeing you up there. Are there any windows in the room you're in?"

I flicked my eyes up to the far wall, where huge windows looked out over the city. "Yeah."

"On how many sides?"

"Just one."

"What can you see from there?"

"We're the tallest building here. The harbour, maybe the roof of the Vodafone building next door."

"Okay, yes. I know the one. I'm going to need you to stay on the opposite end of that room, and keep below the window line, okay? Stay out of sight. That's really important. Nobody can know you're up there. And… this next request might not be easy, but for now, I need you to keep this quiet from everyone. Even your family. I'm sorry I need to ask that from you, but nobody can know you're up there. Just until we get this under control. If it gets out to the media you're up there, things are going to get… complicated."

I looked up at the rest of them. I knew they wouldn't like what he'd said because I didn't either. "You're saying we can't tell our families we're here? What are we supposed to tell them?"

He was silent for a moment. "I'm sorry but, we just can't risk… for now just say what you need to say, but nobody can know where you…"

"Look, I get this is serious but, I'm sorry, we're not dying up here without telling our…"

"Woah! Look, none of you are dying today, okay? That's my job. I'm going to make sure of it. I've just seen the building plans. I wouldn't ask you to stay up there if I didn't think it was your safest option. But if anyone finds out you're up there, things get a lot more complicated for us. So we need you to keep it quiet for now, okay? We've got every available officer on this, including our armed and special forces. The best guys in the country. We'll get you out of there. But we need your help on this, alright?"

I flicked my eyes warily at Steven Black. Chocolate listened with watchful eyes. Sienna was sitting hunched on the floor, staring at the ground between her knees. Darsh sat at one of the tables, staring into nothing. "Yeah. I got it."

"Okay, good. Now I need you to keep this phone free. I'll be in touch often. If you need to make phone calls, try doing it from another phone. How's your battery looking?"

"It's about halfway, sir."

"Okay, that's fine. Keep it open. I'll call you again soon. I'll be right there on the ground in a few minutes. I'm going to give you back to Toni now, and she's going to take a few more details down, like some extra phone numbers and your names and so on. Alright? We're going to get you out of there. Believe me, I won't stop until we do. That's my word."

I said thanks, but my voice croaked and barely a sound came out. The operator lady came back on and asked for more details about us. By now, all the others had huddled against the back wall, talking quietly among themselves.

Then, as I was reciting first and last names to the police lady, the building shook. It was sudden, and we froze and gaped at each other, instantly braced with bent knees, like the earth was shaking. The rumble boomed through the building and vibrated violently through the bottoms of our feet and continued for several long seconds before finally dissipating into a terrifying silence.

"Was that a fucking *bomb*?" Steven Black seethed. He ran for the door and Chocolate followed.

"No!"

They both stopped and turned to me.

"The police guy said to stay in here. Stay out of sight."

Steven Black looked at me again with those burning eyes. Then with a grimace, he breathed in deeply, once, and then out, and then slowly let go of the door handle. After a tense few seconds, he came back shaking his head, and muttered the four words we'd all been thinking ourselves.

"We're going to die."

Two hours passed. It felt like thirty. We sat still, silent, along the inside wall of the lunchroom.

Chocolate stayed glued to his phone and read out the news headlines as they changed every fifteen minutes.

Shooter attacks Persian restaurant in Auckland CBD.

Five confirmed dead in Victoria Park shooting.

Eleven dead, eighteen injured in Victoria Park shooting, more casualties expected.

Shooter confirmed trapped in Auckland office building.

Multiple shooters suspected to be taking siege in Grant & Woodson tower.

Prime Minister condemns terrorist attack on Persian restaurant in CBD.

Attack on popular Persian restaurant suspected to be racially motivated.

Police unable to enter Grant & Woodson tower amid heavy explosives and shooters.

"Yep, front page in India now, too," he sighed. "We're going to be famous. Dead, and famous."

"This is bullshit," Steven Black said, staring at the ceiling. "I need to tell my parents. How can they expect us to hide up here and not tell our families? Let's say this whole building blows up and we didn't tell them? That sound right to you?"

I shrugged. I couldn't say anything. I agreed with him. "I think they just need to make sure it doesn't leak. You know, one person tells another person, the Herald is going to find out eventually. Then we're on the news and…"

"And what? These crazy shooters come running up here to kill us? They're going to do that anyway."

"They don't know we're here," Sienna said softly.

"Of course they know, man, our cars are in the car park. Where else would we be?"

I turned my head and glanced at him. His eyes fumed. Chocolate was the opposite, quiet with anxiety. Sienna stayed silent, but it seemed every time I looked over at her, fresh tears were welling in her eyes. Only Darsh was emotionless.

"You always come in on a Saturday?"

They all looked up at me. I was looking at Darsh. He sighed deeply, then looked back at the ground.

"Nah… I was just getting the boardroom ready for Monday. The partners have a big thing early on Monday morning."

"Oh, that's right…" My mind rolled back to the staff newsletter that week. "That big marketing agency they talked about, yeah?"

He shrugged. "Not sure, man. I just do the tech."

I didn't know a lot about Darsh at the time. That would change immensely over the weekend to come, but before that day I only knew two things about him; he was the IT guy, and he was Indian. And one of those was only half-true.

Darsh had an Indian father but actually grew up in Sri Lanka. To be honest, I didn't know the difference between the two. His lunch smelled and looked just like Indian food, and I suspected it was just as delicious. His skin was dark, his features were sharp, and his accent was a mild mix of Indian and Kiwi undertones. He seemed reasonably well put-together, always in a well-fitted suit, and the shirt always matched the tie. And people liked him well enough. That was probably the most telling thing about him; I'd never heard anyone in that office say a single bad thing about Darsh.

Part of that could've been because we never saw him. Or rather, we saw him often – in the server room, in the IT office, carrying computers and screens and projectors around the office – we just never got the chance to talk to him. Any time we crossed paths, we simply swapped a 'Morning, bro' or 'Hey, what's up', and coming to think of it, those were possibly the only five words we'd said to each other in three whole years.

My phone rang. I recognised the number.

"How you doing, son? Superintendent Delowe."

"Yeah, we're uh. Getting along."

"Listen, we're not sure how long you're going to be up there. But as you can imagine, this is a complex thing we're dealing with. I just want you to know we're working as hard and as fast as we can. I can promise you; I'm not going home to sleep until you're down here with me."

His voice was different now. Calmer, but with more concern. I guess he'd just needed a moment to come to grips with it, like us. Either way, he seemed sincere.

"Thanks. We appreciate it."

"Anyway, here's the situation. We've shut the power off in the building. And like I told you before, the lifts and access card system are off too. We're trying to give them as little resources and movement as possible. But we still need to be able to contact you guys. You got any power banks or laptops or anything you can use to keep your phones charged?"

I managed a smirk. "I think one of us can sort that out."

"Hey, Darsh. We need to get some laptops together so we can keep our phones charged. Can you hook that up?"

Without saying anything, he stood up and walked calmly out of the room. The IT office was just next door.

"Just a reminder if anyone leaves that room, make sure they stay under the window line. You might have to crawl around, I'm afraid."

I thought about calling out before he got too far, but stopped myself, remembering there were no windows in the hallway. Barely two minutes passed before he came in rolling an equipment cart with around fifteen laptops on it. Even Chocolate managed a snicker.

"I think we're good for laptops, officer."

"Okay, now the water is still on, for fire safety, mostly. So you should be fine for water. But do you have any food up there?"

I looked over at the pantry, the staff fridge, the drinks fridge we'd emptied the night before, the door to Chef Margot's kitchen. "I think we'll be... okay."

And for the next thirty minutes, we ransacked Chef Margot's kitchen. It was the first time any of us had been in there. The freezer was mostly big cuts of meat and some ice, but she also had several bags of frozen scones and hamburger buns. The fridge was more fruitful, with a decent stash of bread and milk, fruits, raisins and berries and chocolate chips, plus a few boxes of half-eaten cake.

The lunchroom pantry had the usual coffee, tea, sugars, and a whole shelf of Friday night bags of pretzels. The staff fridge was mostly boxes of questionable leftovers and pre-packed lunches and random condiments. And, of course, the bottom half of the drinks fridge was still full of Coke and L&P.

We laid it all out on the lunchroom bench and I counted everything out, bouncing my finger and whispering *one-two-three-four-five* under my breath.

"Eleven bags of pretzels, sixteen bottles of red wine, nine bottles of white, twenty-six Cokes, sixteen Sprites, eleven Fantas, ten L&P's."

Next was the haul from Chef Margot.

"Three litres of milk, twelve bananas, four apples, some grapes, six cans of pineapples, four cans of condensed milk, one can of cherries, half a chocolate cake, half a carrot cake, three bags of raisins, a bag of chocolate chips, two bags of frozen berries, one block of butter, two bags of cheese, tin of flour, tin of sugar, two bottles of cream."

Then the staff fridge and pantry.

"Two jars of peanut butter, some leftover spaghetti, Thomas M's two slices of pizza, six different boxes of cereal, Matt L's frozen bag of bagels, Blonde Amy's salad from Subway, four frozen loaves of bread, and one tub of half-eaten mint chocolate chip..."

"Ice cream!" Sienna grinned. I hadn't seen her smile in a few hours. "We could probably survive the month," she said, staring at it all.

"No way. Chocolate can eat all of this in a day."

We all looked at him and chuckled, but he wasn't in the mood for jokes. Just gave us the straight-lipped smile and nodded, silently.

"The power's out, so we've got to keep the fridge closed. Let's keep the milk and cream and cake in there and finish that first. Then I guess the bread and fruit next. And pretzels and peanut butter and that kind of stuff, eat that last."

"And the ice cream tonight," Sienna said, holding the tub to her chest.

"You guys are talking like we're gonna be in here 'til Christmas," Steven Black scoffed.

I turned my palms up, shrugging a shoulder. "Best to be safe, I guess."

"Well, let's rip into these bananas now then!" he said, grabbing a bunch. He broke one off and threw it at me. Then went to throw one at Chocolate, who shook his head. Sienna did too. And Darsh. Steven Black shrugged and took one for himself, and we all retreated back to the same lunchroom wall we'd been sitting against all afternoon.

That evening, just before darkness fell, Superintendent Delowe called again. He asked to be put on speaker, and we all huddled around the phone and listened eagerly.

The first thing he told us; we'd probably be staying the night up there. There were devices they suspected were bombs wired at all three entrances, and he couldn't get a bomb squad close enough. Shots were still being fired whenever they approached the building.

The second thing he told us; after looking at the building plans, we could leave the lunchroom, but only to the two meeting rooms and IT office down that hallway, and to the boardroom across the hall. Anywhere else would expose us to windows. Media cameras were everywhere, and we couldn't risk them seeing us. If we had to go anywhere else in the building, to get a laptop to charge the phone, for example, he said to crawl 'like in the army', and for only one of us to go. But he made it clear, at least three or four times – only for 'absolute emergencies'.

The third thing he told us; be quiet. He wasn't sure exactly where the suspects were in the building and, especially at night, there'd be a chance they could hear us. "Talk in whispers, and walk on eggshells."

The fourth thing he told us; we couldn't go into the stairwell to use the toilet. He asked us, regretfully, to piss in the sink, and to gather some of the small rubbish bins from around the office for 'number twos'. He suggested each of us get one for ourselves and designate a 'toilet room' to keep them in. We all cringed at the sound of it, but since there was a mini kitchenette in the boardroom, we decided instantly that would be the 'shitting and pissing-in-the-sink' room. Nobody but the partners ever saw the inside of that room, anyway. We figured this would be a perfect way to christen it for the East Side.

The fifth thing he told us; don't sleep alone. We should all sleep in a room with at least one other person, and ideally all together. It was important we all knew where each other was at any one time. We told him we doubted we'd be sleeping at all. He managed a laugh and said he wouldn't be either.

The sixth thing he told us; he was sorry. And that he'd worked his whole life to be prepared for a moment like this, and he'd be stopping at nothing to get us back to our families.

"He actually seems alright," Steven Black said after we hung up.

We sat tired, silent, in a circle on the lunchroom floor. The sun had long set, and now only moonlight lit the room through the large windows on the far wall. In the centre lay a pile of banana peels, a handful of dirty spoons inside the ice cream tub, two empty bread bags, an empty cake box, and a jar of peanut butter. Beside us, we each had a Coke, except for Sienna, who crinkled an empty L&P can between her fingers.

"You guys wanna see what's happening outside?" she said.

We all looked at her, confused.

"But we can't…"

"I know somewhere…" she interrupted. "He just said stay away from windows, right? So nobody sees us?"

She put her L&P down and stood up slowly. None of us moved or said anything, just watched her tiptoe, like a ballet dancer, over Chocolate and Darsh's legs and then to the door. She pulled the handle down and it creaked ever so softly, but the room was so silent, it felt like we could hear the sound whirl past us and echo across the room. As she was about to step out, she turned and looked at us, all sitting on the floor like kindergarten kids, staring right back at her.

"C'mon!" she whispered.

We followed her, crawling single file across the hallway, past the entrance of the boardroom, which opened out into the reception waiting area. It felt like we were twelve-year-olds again, sneaking out of our cabins during school camp, the eeriness causing me to shiver like we were trespassing and might be caught any second. I'd never been in the office this dark, this quiet. I almost doubted these were the same floors I'd spent the last few years walking across every day.

The client waiting area was made up of four colourful couches, surrounding an oversized coffee table. I cringed at the moonlight pouring in through the windows at reception, just a few metres away. But a thin three-quarter wall separated the reception desk from the waiting area, which kept us all hidden. That wall was also lined with magazine racks and a water cooler and little baskets of shortbread cookies and breath mints we'd all forgotten about. As we crawled past, I reached up and grabbed both, sure to add them to our food stash in the lunchroom. Then, at the front of the waiting area stood a huge floor-to-ceiling window, looking out over the entirety of Victoria Park. It was the same window I'd found Sienna at that afternoon, in those moments after hearing the first gunshots.

Sienna stood up and walked over to it, her face only an inch from the glass. I was seconds from launching to my feet and tackling her to pull her back down. From the looks of it, Chocolate was too. Yet the calmness with which she did it threw us off, and we stopped ourselves before turning to one another with confused glances.

"This is a double window," she finally whispered. "It's a mirror on the other side. Nobody can see in."

We all gaped at each other, then stood up and shuffled next to her, and with our first glimpse at the street below, our eyes glowed with disbelief. It was filled with police cars and vans, army vehicles, news cameras, important-looking men in suits, flashing blue and red lights, officers in full assault gear – the kind of thing you'd see in *Call of Duty* – orange cones lining the intersections in every direction, two ambulances parked side by side, lights flashing. It was hard to believe this was really our street.

My eyes flicked between each face; the reporter talking on his phone with too many hand movements, the two paramedics sitting on the edge of an ambulance, the officer built like a rugby player strolling up and down with a rifle under his armpit. My gaze stopped on a guy sitting on the footpath, just beside a police car, chewing his way through a Subway sandwich. Meatball, I guessed. He looked like he'd been there all day, the way his shoulders slumped slightly, his tie hung loose, his hair cleanly combed at the back but falling slightly messy at the front. Then suddenly his head popped, and he turned to look somewhere in the distance before jumping to his feet and jogging over. An older officer handed him a radio, and he listened intently. I wondered if that was Superintendent Delowe, and tried to match his voice to the face. I shrugged. Maybe.

Steven Black broke the silence. "It's like a movie," he whispered, hands resting on his hips. "Like *Die Hard*, man. You know that scene? That black dude with the donuts camped outside the building, trying to figure out what Bruce Willis is doing?"

We all heard him, but nobody said anything. It was too much to take in, too hard to believe this was the same road we walked down every morning and evening. For so long, we'd considered this the most boring street in the city. Nobody came here for anything. Nothing newsworthy ever happened here. And now, suddenly, everything did.

That night, we all slept in the lunchroom. The back wall was lined with a padded bench, the kind you'd find in a McDonald's booth. Steven Black fell asleep there first. Darsh fell asleep next, just a few inches down. Sienna slept on the floor in the corner, her purse and sweater stuffed under her head like a pillow.

I didn't sleep. I sat upright, my back against the south wall, the same one we'd been sitting against all day. My throat tickled, and I looked over at the fridge and thought about getting another Coke. It gave me flashes of that morning, where we'd been in Chocolate's car, down on the waterfront, knocking down beers we'd stolen from the very same fridge. Eighteen hours later, here we were again. Right back where we'd started.

It must have been about 3 a.m. when I finally gave up on sleeping. I crinkled the empty Coke can between my palms, a habit I'd had since I was young, but stopped myself, mindful it might wake someone, or that the crazy shooter person might hear it through the floorboards. I looked over at Darsh snoring with envy. My eyes were wide open, sucking in moonlight, now doubly wide with caffeine and sugar. I snuck out the door and crawled back to the window at reception.

To my surprise, Chocolate was sitting there, cross-legged, staring at the road below. I hadn't noticed he was gone. I crawled up next to him, slid up close to the glass and hugged my knees to my chest. We both gazed silently at the scene below as if looking down on an ant farm. Nothing much had changed. It was quieter, slightly, maybe because things had settled a bit. The shots had continued sporadically throughout that day, but we hadn't heard one in several hours.

"You know… I've never heard a gunshot before," I said quietly.

"Really?"

"Yeah."

Chocolate nodded to himself, his eyes still fixed on the road below. "Me neither."

The officer eating the Subway sandwich was still there. Although the sandwich was finished and had been replaced by a takeaway coffee cup. I guessed it was from the gas station down the road, where we sometimes bought pies on Friday nights.

"Didn't really sound the same as in the movies, right?" I asked.

He shook his head, in slow motion, five, six times, as if reliving the noises in his mind. "Nah…" Then he shook his head again, faster this time. "Nah, man. Shucks. Way different."

I let out a breath, a long one, and looked around at the ceiling, as if there were answers or comfort waiting for me up there. "All those times we talked about how we didn't want to spend any more of our lives in this place." I managed half a smile, thinking over the many mornings I'd ridden up that elevator, promising myself that soon it would be my last. "Now… we're probably gonna die in here."

We both laughed, doing our best to keep it hushed. They weren't happy laughs, obviously. But we needed some laughing, or some crying. And neither of us felt like crying, yet.

"You know what, man? I wish you weren't here, but… I'm happy you're here, you know? Like if we're gonna survive this, you're the one I'd choose to survive it with. I can think of a lot worse people to die with in here."

I held out my fist. He bumped it.

"Fuck, imagine if you were stuck in here with Drewlove."

"Yeah, or…"

"Georgina!" We both laughed again. A real laugh, this time.

"I mean, I know we all die, and if I die next to you, then alright. But I just wish it'd happened when we're eighty, on a beach somewhere. Instead of in this fucking place."

"Well," I offered. "It wasn't the worst life, really. Was it? I mean, free beer on Friday, and Chef Margot's raspberry cheesecake, and…"

We stayed silent and thought for a moment.

"Can't think of anything else, actually."

"Me neither," he laughed.

"Everyone asleep?"

"Yeah. Steve's in a mood, but he knocked out. Darsh, fast asleep. Sienna…"

"Yeah, how's she doing? You guys are pretty close, right?"

"She seems okay. Might be doing the best out of all of us, actually."

"Yeah?"

"She found us this window, didn't she? She's an artist. Probably sees beauty or poetry in everything, you know. Including this."

"She'll probably write a book about it."

"Oh man, this would make one hell of a play."

He turned and crinkled his eyebrows at me. "Play?"

And just before he said it, I smiled to myself, remembering, and shook my head. "Nothing."

Sunday

I woke up on one of the couches in reception. It was a smell that woke me up. That seemed odd because if there was one place in that entire office they kept sparkling clean, it was the waiting area in reception. I sniffed the couch, which smelled somewhat like an aeroplane pillow. Not my favourite smell, but hardly offensive. I sniffed the magazines on the coffee table. They smelled like paper. I knelt down and smelled the rug under the coffee table. Musky, like a grandmother's knitting. But not offensive either. Then I sniffed the air, and that led my nose to my shoulder, and then my armpit. And then I realised. Of course. The smell was coming from me.

I knelt down and crawled into the hallway towards the lunchroom. I could hear the whispers in there, even from around the corner, though when I finally stepped inside, I barely recognised it. It looked like we'd been living in there for a month.

Sienna had found garbage bags in Chef Margot's kitchen, and I saw one stashed in the corner, already ballooning with banana peels and Coke cans and takeaway boxes and empty bread bags. Staying below the window line meant we always sat on the floor, in a circle, and they all sat in the same spot as the day before, now glugging cups of milk and chomping on peanut butter sandwiches. Sienna was crouched in the middle, making one of her own.

"Breakfast?" She smiled as I sat down, handing it to me.

I was still only half awake. "Thanks."

Chocolate had half a banana in his hand and was reading out news articles again.

With 29 now confirmed dead, and several still unaccounted for, the Pride of Persia massacre is set to become the deadliest public shooting in New Zealand's history.

I heard the words, but I wasn't trying to hear any more headlines. I could tell he'd been reading articles aloud all morning because everybody else had tuned out as well.

Then Sienna finally stood up and rested her hands on her hips. "Can I say something?"

We all stopped eating and looked up at her.

"I'm sorry, but I'm just going to say it." She looked at me first. Hesitated, then looked at Chocolate. And finally Steven Black. "You guys smell."

I let out a wry smile and nodded at her.

"We've been in these clothes since Friday morning," I said grimly. "And we had a hell of a Friday night."

Steven Black's eyes turned upwards as he replayed the memory, smiling.

"Well, unfortunately, we don't keep a wardrobe at our little cubicles," Chocolate mumbled, still scrolling through his phone.

My eyes lit up. "But someone does!"

Chocolate squinted at me as if the answer was written on my forehead in fine print. "Ohh! Yeah!"

He stuffed the rest of the banana into his mouth and threw the peel at the garbage bag in the corner, missing it by half a mile. Then picked himself off the floor and walked with me to the door.

"Okay, but look," I said, resting my hand on the door handle. "We're not supposed to be going down there."

"Delowe said we could go to get supplies. For emergencies."

"Yeah, but is this an emergency?"

"Yes," Sienna said from across the room. "It is. Go."

Chocolate and I eyeballed each other, trying not to smile.

"Okay, but we gotta be stealth!"

"Shucks mate, I was born stealth."

"You're a fucking hippo."

"And you're what, a sloth?"

"Just follow me, and don't get us killed."

We tiptoed down the hallway, then fell to all fours and crawled past the elevators. But each time our knees hit the ground, I could almost hear the floor echo and winced with nervousness.

"Shhh!" I whispered back at Chocolate.

"It's you!" he seethed back at me.

At the pace we moved, it felt like we'd be crawling until sundown. We got to the West Side entrance and sat up against the wall to rest. With the air conditioning off, beads of sweat rolled down both our foreheads. After catching our breath, we crawled past the filing room and into the West Side. Now that we had to avoid them, the windows on the West Side seemed twice as large and bright as I'd remembered. I dropped to my stomach and army-crawled, moving only inches at a time. I glanced back at Chocolate. He was doing the same.

It took us forever to get to Drewlove's office. Luckily, the door was already open. The office doors were huge and moving them could have easily been caught by a camera from the ground. Though we figured we were just being paranoid, and the chance of someone zooming in on that particular office window was close to zero. Still, I told Chocolate to stay outside. I was much smaller than him and was able to crawl in and get to Drewlove's closet without much trouble.

We'd seen his small collection of shirts and ties in there several times, and never thought much of it. Just found it bizarre how he kept them there, since we'd never seen him change shirts at the office, ever. At least now, his little collection would finally have a purpose.

When I finally weaselled my way out, with great difficulty, a handful of shirts thrown over my shoulder, we sat behind his secretary's desk and flicked through them.

Chocolate gave an approving nod. "Not bad."

"You reckon all these other partners got clothes too?"

He pursed his lips, holding up one of Drewlove's shirts. "Let's find out."

By the time we army-crawled back into the lunchroom an hour later, we had enough fancy shirts to start our own High Street store. Not to mention a few pairs of pants, a couple of blazers, and three bottles of cologne from Peter Mack's desk.

"We were about to come looking for you!" Sienna glared at us.

"Good things take time," Chocolate said, grinning.

We laid the clothes out over one of the tables.

"Check this out!" Steven Black gasped, flicking through them. "Burberry. Saint Laurent. Whose are these?"

"Eugene's."

"High roller. Life of a West Sider, eh?"

Sam Drewlove's shirts were more my size, though his were hardly as glamorous. Barkers, mostly. Not that I was complaining. Any clean shirt was a treat.

Once we'd picked our spoils, the four boys headed to Chef Margot's kitchen. We laughed hopelessly as we gave ourselves a wash with some dishwashing soap and paper towels and changed into our fresh wardrobe.

As we came out, Sienna tried to cover her mouth but couldn't stop herself from laughing out loud. "All partners now, huh?" She giggled like a big sister watching her brothers play dress-up.

Eugene's shirts actually fit Steven Black perfectly. With a little haircut, you might have guessed he was getting ready for a modelling shoot. "Can't forget the scent." He grinned, heading back to the table and walking his fingers over the cologne bottles. "Peter Mack eh, living the high life. What you reckon boys, DKNY? Dior?"

We each picked up a bottle and sprayed profusely. I'd never worn cologne in my life, but suddenly felt inclined – indulging in a first-time experience, with death lingering on the doorstep.

"Okay, enough, enough! You boys are… ugh." She waved her hands across her face, reeling from the smell. We all grinned at each other.

"How do we smell now?"

"Fantastic," she said, rolling her eyes. "Just… fantastic."

It seemed our little clothing mission had lifted our spirits some, perhaps even got the adrenaline pumping, and by mid-afternoon, the shock of our situation was starting to wear off. At least some of it. Steven Black was no longer moping, Chocolate's eyes had come back to life, and Sienna's heartwarming rabbit-toothed smile was shining brightly once again. Darsh and Chocolate had even opened up one of the laptops and were playing video games. We'd heard about three sets of gunshots during the day, and by the third set, nobody even stopped to look at each other anymore. Perhaps the alcohol stash had something to do with it, too.

I was lying on the seats against the back wall with Steven Black and Sienna, picking at pretzels and wine. They were both on their third glass, at least.

"Anyone from work texted you?" I asked.

Steven Black nodded. "Tons."

"Anyone ask where you are?"

"Dad…" Steven Black mumbled.

"Boyfriend," Sienna followed.

"What you tell 'em?"

"Studying with a friend."

"Studying at home."

My girlfriend had been texting non-stop as well. "That's your building! Oh my god!" I'd tried to stay nonchalant, even said I was semi-happy about it. Work would be closed; I could study from home for a while. "Big workshop next week," I'd said. It wasn't that easy to build a lie around it, but it hadn't bothered me, to be honest; I knew I could explain everything later.

"Yo, Chocolate. Your family ask where you are?"

"Yeah," he said, his eyes fixated on the screen. "Oh, man! How you always kill me like that?" He punched Darsh on the arm, and they both snickered at each other.

"What you tell 'em?"

He finally turned away from the screen and looked at me. "I said I was with you."

"Doing what?"

"Road tripping."

I laughed sadly. "If only. I'd kill for one of those chicken and veggies right now. Hamilton trip if we ever get outta here, eh?"

"Shucks mate, Hawaii trip, more like it!" he bellowed, jamming the laptop keys.

"Guys, shhhh!" Sienna leered at us. "We're supposed to be whispering, remember? Murderer downstairs? Got a gun? Might come up here and kill us all? Yeah?"

We smiled sheepishly. She was right. Somehow, we'd almost forgotten why we were here.

A few seconds later, Chocolate's phone started vibrating. Still engrossed in his game with Darsh, he turned his eyes down for a split second and stared at the screen.

"It's Jeff."

I walked over to look. "Answer it?"

"Nah, man. Then I just need to lie to him too. I can't keep up with all these lies."

"Just tell him what you told everyone else. We're road tripping."

Chocolate shook his head, laughing. "He'll ask why we didn't invite him."

Then the call cut, and not two seconds later, Steven Black's phone started vibrating. He snatched it off the table, frowned, and held it up to us. "Jeff."

"Maybe it's something important?"

Chocolate laughed. "Mate, when has Jeff ever called you about anything important?"

"Well, maybe that's why he's calling us all?"

I watched his name flash on the screen from a distance, three times, four times, five times. Then, just before it stopped, Steven Black shook his head as well.

"Choc's right. I love ol' Jeff, but I ain't got energy to be spouting lies to him as well."

Then, as I'd feared, my phone rang next. "Shiiiiiit," I whispered, pulling my phone from my pocket. But it wasn't Jeffery. It was Superintendent Delowe. I put him on speaker, and we huddled around.

"How you all doin'? Alright?"

We all grunted.

"Yeah, well, can't blame ya. Look, good news and bad news, I'm afraid. Good news first, yeah?" He didn't wait for us to answer. "Good news is, we think we know who's in there. We've traced his car through the city's CCTV, and we think we know. We're quite sure we know. I want you to know we're making progress, and we're on it. Bad news… we still can't get in there. He's rigged the place up pretty good. Until we can get a bomb squad up to the points of entry for long enough, we can't be sending men in. He's still in there shooting. We can't risk any more lives than we need to. At this stage, it's looking like we might end up having to starve him out. So…" He took a long breath, then sighed. "So it looks like you might be up there another night."

Nobody said anything. Nobody looked at each other. We just picked at a fingernail, rubbed a chin, scratched the back of our neck. There was nothing else we could do.

"How you guys for food? You okay?"

Everybody hummed, muttering under their breath. Darsh had already gone back to his video game.

"Yeah," I said finally. "We'll be okay."

"I'm sorry, guys. I really am. We're going to get you out of there. Hang in there for me, alright?"

As soon as he hung up, Steven Black grabbed the bottle and swigged it hard. "This is such bullshit, man. Just drive a tank through the front and cook him! What's so hard about that? It's one fucking guy!"

"It's all politics, man." I shook my head. "You know, if they do some Rambo stuff and an officer dies, then someone loses their job. They look like shit in the newspaper. That kind of thing. People's careers are probably riding on this thing. They gotta look perfect an' whatever."

"Man, screw their careers. How about not getting *us* killed, how about that?"

"That too."

"If he calls tomorrow and says we have *another* day in here," Steven Black said, grimacing, "I say we run down those stairs and cook this loser ourselves."

"Cook him, eh? How do we do that, Black?"

"Just walk right up to him, strangle his face off."

"Strangle his bullets, too?"

"Yes, man! Or I promise you, I'm gonna do *something*. Better than sitting up here waiting to get blown up. Isn't it?"

He grabbed the bottle of wine and sucked down a few gulps. He was normally a cheery person, Steven Black, but he'd been on edge ever since we'd heard those first shots that morning when we'd bounced off these very same seats into reception, half-eaten croissants hanging out of our mouths. And as we watched him now, drinking angrily from the bottle, we weren't sure if it was the sudden outburst, the tight-fitting purple shirt, or the ridiculous amount of high-end cologne emanating from his body, but we all suddenly burst into laughter at the sight of him. He peered down at us in fits, and then, after a devil's stare that lasted less than a second, coughed up half a mouthful of wine and started rolling with laughter himself.

As soon as the sun started to fall, we ended up back in our usual circle on the floor, laying out dinner once again in the centre. As the electricity was shut off, the building fell into darkness as soon as sundown arrived. We got a few hours of fading sunlight during dusk, but after that, our only light was the moonlight that filtered in from the windows on the far wall and the torches on our phones.

"I think we need to ration this food better," Sienna said, tying up another bag of garbage. "It's only the second day, and we've finished all the bread and peanut butter."

It was hard to believe it had only been that long. Somehow, it was starting to feel like we'd been living there for weeks.

"Look at all this cereal though," Steven Black grinned, shovelling another spoonful of muesli into his mouth.

"And how long will that last?" Sienna quipped back, raising her eyebrows. "One more day?"

"Nah, man. If Chocolate stops eating that Nutri-Grain all the time, should last us the whole week!"

"That's because he eats them straight out of the box, like chips." I laughed to myself, one slow chuckle after another. I could barely sit upright against the wall, holding my belly from too many sandwiches. "He does that at his desk, too."

"They taste better that way."

"Okay, I'm going to divide all the rest of this food up into seven days," Sienna declared like she was suddenly the matron of the house. "It's bad enough we're at risk of getting killed by a madman. I don't want to worry about dying of starvation too."

"And what if we're in here longer than seven days, genius?" Steven Black snarled before tipping the rest of the muesli into his mouth.

She smiled mockingly. "Then we die."

"Geez, what happened to fun Sienna?" He put his bowl down and came to slouch against the wall beside me. "Going a little coo-coo in here, huh?"

"Not a little coo-coo. Totally coo-coo!"

"And what if it goes the other way? What if we don't make it seven days?" I was still massaging my stomach like it might burst any second. My eyes were closed now, and I talked in a half-asleep drawl. "Let's say this guy blows this whole building up tomorrow. We'll have deprived ourselves of our last few bowls of Nutri-Grain… all for nothing."

"Oooooh see… it's a tough call, Sienna," Chocolate said, laughing. "You willing to bear that guilt for the rest of your life? Any time I see you in heaven, I won't let you forget it."

"Who says you're going to heaven?" Steven Black laughed.

"Shucks, mate, I'm probably the only one in here going to heaven!"

My eyes popped open suddenly, and Sienna and I jeered at him.

"What about me?"

"And me?"

Chocolate scoffed. "Do you guys even go to church?"

We all nodded vigorously.

"I went last year, on Christmas."

"I went when my grandma died."

"My brother got married in a church, and I was in the front row."

"Y'all sinners ain't going anywhere near heaven!"

Darsh interrupted from behind his laptop screen. "What about me? I go to the temple. Every week."

"There you go," Chocolate said proudly, pointing. "Me and Darsh, then! Me and Darsh will be eating Nutri-Grain in heaven. The rest of y'all, better eat now while you can."

"Sounds good to me," Steven Black said, crawling toward the cereal boxes.

"No!" Sienna cried, then covered her mouth quickly, realising how loud she'd been. "No. Seriously. We're on rations now."

Steven Black sighed but relented. He knew it was a good idea. We all did.

"But we have plenty of Coke and wine," she said, pointing to the drinks. "If you're hungry, drink."

"Even better!" He crawled over to the alcohol stash, grabbed two bottles of wine and opened both, swigged one, then passed them around. "For all we know, we'll be dead by morning. Let's enjoy it."

The wine made that night move quickly. I slouched on the large couch in reception, the same one I'd slept on the night before, and stared out the double window several metres away. It must have been close to midnight. Though my eyes were barely half open, I basked in the night sky opening out in front of me. I knew the other side of that window was still far, far away, but it soothed, at least in glimpses.

As my eyes began to close for good, my phone rang for the third time in an hour. I already knew it was my girlfriend; Superintendent Delowe never called that late. I muted it and threw it on the chair beside me, then drank another glug from the bottle.

Seconds later, Sienna came in and found me staring into the blackness. "Timing out?" she asked.

"Aren't we all in time out?"

She sat down beside me and grabbed the wine from my hand, swigged it, and handed it back to me.

"Can't sleep?" I asked.

She shook her head.

It was silent for a moment. Long, but not long enough to be awkward. I took another sip.

"How much do you think this wine costs?" I asked, holding the bottle up in front of me. My hand cupped the base, and I squeezed it, wondering how much harder I'd need to squeeze until it broke.

"No idea," she said, glancing at the name. "What's it called?"

"Mud House."

She pulled out her phone.

"No, don't Google it. Just guess, what you reckon?"

"I don't know. I never drink wine, really."

"Me neither."

I swigged it again and twirled the bottle in my hands. "I'm gonna say… fifteen dollars."

"Really?"

"What, is that too high or too low?"

"I was going to say maybe eight dollars."

"You can buy wine for eight dollars?"

"You can buy wine for four dollars."

I looked at the label again, studying the 'M' on the Mud House, trying to decode it as if I'd never seen a wine label before. I'd seen many, of course, but this might have been the first time I'd ever looked at one. "I've never bought a bottle of wine in my life. It tastes like cough syrup, man. I just drink it 'cause I dunno, the boys pull out the bottle and it's like, you want a glass? So I say, yeah, sure. But I mean, do people actually like this? Surely people don't think this tastes better than, say, Fanta." I swigged again and handed it to her. She took a short sip and nodded.

"Yeah, pineapple Fanta, oh! So much better than this." She sipped it again. "Why don't they get pineapple Fanta for us on Fridays? And passionfruit! That's the best one."

"Just orange, eh?"

"Just orange. That's the worst one."

"I wonder why they do that. They all cost the same, right?"

"I think so."

"Add that to the list of shit we need to ask for when this is over. Pineapple Fanta on Fridays."

My phone vibrated again. We both flicked our eyes across and stared at it. I watched it *rrrr* twice, three, four times. Then I looked back at the bottle. I had to admit, it was a pretty nice-looking M. "Do you miss your boyfriend?" I asked.

She sucked her lips in and looked at the ceiling for a moment, then sighed. "Yeah. I guess I do." She took a longer drink this time, then handed me the bottle. "Do you miss your girlfriend?"

My eyes gazed far out the window, over to the twinkling lights across the harbour. "Not really."

She laughed, and I laughed with her.

"Well," I said, rethinking. "Define 'miss'."

She exhaled, leaned forward to lift her hair off her back, before falling back against the seat. "I guess… if you miss someone, it means you would rather be somewhere with them, rather than where you are right now."

I sipped the wine again, and feeling the lightness of the bottle, tipped it all the way up until it was finished. "How did you end up here, anyway? You don't belong here."

She shrugged. "It's a job. What about you? If you hate it so much, how did *you* end up here?"

"I don't hate it."

"You do!"

"I don't *hate* it. It's just… it's so meaningless, you know? You come here every day in this stupid-looking shirt, and you do taxes for all these rich people who don't give a shit about it, then at the end, you give them this little folder with ten pieces of paper, and they pay us $20,000."

"And then you get $1,000 of it." She laughed.

"Yeah, and you get $800."

"Please," she scoffed. "I don't even get close to $800 of it."

"Yeah, and I don't even get close to $1,000."

"Well, at least we get a fifteen-dollar bottle of wine on Friday."

"Eight-dollar bottle of wine."

"Four-dollar bottle of wine!"

We both laughed.

She took the empty bottle from me and threw it up and down lightly, spinning it between her hands. "So… if you could leave this place and go anywhere else…" she trailed off. "Anywhere at all. If you could swap lives with anyone. Where would you go?"

I looked at her, blank for a moment. "Good question…" It had been a while since anyone had asked me a question I actually cared enough to think about. "You know… you inspired me, actually."

"Me?"

"Yeah."

"How?"

"You know, on Friday, when I saw your book. *A Streetcar Named Desire*. I just kept thinking about it that night, and the next day…" I stared out the window as I talked like I was talking to the sky, and she was just watching our conversation like an audience member at a talk show. "It reminded me of when I was a kid. There was this show I used to watch. It was called *Boy Meets World*. You heard of it?"

"No."

"Maybe it's a few years before you. But it was just this stupid show about this nerdy kid in high school. And I used to watch it every day. It used to come on right before Full House.

"I love that show!"

"Yeah, and it's not like I looked forward to it all day or anything, but I was just always in front of the TV when it came on, and I loved it for some reason, I couldn't not watch it. Then one day I saw an interview with some of the cast, the main guy, his name was Cory in the show, I don't know what his real name was. And I was probably… I don't know, maybe twelve or thirteen back then, and I saw this guy doing an interview, and he wasn't Cory anymore! That's when I realised, hey, this guy's actually a real person. I mean, I always knew the show wasn't real, but somehow it still felt real. And then they showed some bloopers, like behind the scenes and stuff. It looked like so much fun. I was amazed. These guys' job is to create a new world and pretend to be a totally different person and look how fun it looks! And for the longest time, that's what I wanted to do. I wanted to be an actor."

"So why didn't you?"

"Because I didn't know I could. I always thought you go to school, and you choose the subjects you want to do at school and that becomes your job. I mean, they give you a list of subjects at school, right? And on that list it's got history, English, maths, it even has sport. But it doesn't have acting. I thought all those actors, they didn't go to high school, they went to some other special school or something."

165

"That's so stupid."

"Yeah and, okay don't laugh, but…" I didn't want to look at her in case she did laugh. So I looked at my fingernails. A piece of skin was peeling around the edge. I picked at it softly. "I never realised it wasn't like that until I talked to you on Friday."

"Like what?"

"Like, if you want to do something, you just go and do it. I just assumed I never learned 'acting' so I'm not allowed to do it. Like all these kids on TV, they must have learned to act growing up, right? At some special acting school. And I never did. I went to normal school. So I'm not allowed, but they are."

She laughed a proper laugh this time. "*Allowed*. Like you get a permission slip or something."

"Yeah."

"So, after all this is over. You gonna be an actor?"

"Nah."

"Why not?"

"I don't know how."

"Geez. You haven't learned anything."

"No! I have. I don't think I want to be an actor anymore. But I want to do something."

"So answer my question then."

"What question?"

"If you could swap lives with anyone…"

166

"Oh…" I looked at the ceiling, blubbing my lips over and over. "Well… I saw this video the other day. This Australian guy. He grows rice. Used to grow rice in Aussie, but he lives in Cambodia now, grows rice on some farm out there. Then after the harvest, he loads it up onto trucks, takes it around to all the families who don't have food. There was some war there or something, now heaps of families don't have food. So that's what he does. He just grows rice, sells a little bit, then gives away all the rest to feed people."

"So you wanna be a rice farmer?"

"Nah! Man. I dunno. I just want to do something that matters to someone. I mean, I gotta get out of this city first of all, and then do something, you know. Something cool. When's the last time you did something cool?" I grabbed the bottle back off her and pressed it between my palms. "Well, actually I guess for you, it's different because you're already doing something cool. This office here, you're just passing through, you know? You haven't dedicated half your life to it like we have. So when you're done, you're going to write and entertain people and all that. And one day you're going to have your own book. *A Schoolbus Named Admire. By Sienna Sutton Walsh. New York Times number one bestseller. Now on Broadway. All shows sold out. Time 100 Most Influential Person 2025. The pride of New Zealand.*"

She smiled slowly. "Optimistic."

"I'm jealous, you know. You've got something you love, and you're doing it. You could make something that matters to people."

"What makes you think that? Nobody in this city goes to watch plays. How many people in this city do you know who have gone to see a play?"

"You know…" I sat up and chuckled. "I'll admit, I don't even really know what a play is. I mean, of course I know what it is, but… is it just the same as those things we did in primary school?"

"See?" She laughed. "I don't think people care about what I do any more than they care about what you do."

"To be honest, Sienna," I said, resting the bottle on the couch between us. "I don't think I've met anyone in this city who cared about anything other than themselves."

We both lay there with our feet up on the coffee table, staring out the window. And then I grabbed the bottle one more time and tipped it to my mouth again, half expecting a sip, even though I knew it was empty.

Part 4

Monday

That morning, the motorways filled up again. The queues outside the coffee shops were back, the Monday morning radio shows blared from car stereos. Downtown, the train station echoed once again with the *tap-tap-tap* of high heels and dress shoes, an ebbing sea of smartly dressed men and women. But this Monday morning was different. This Monday morning, nobody was talking about the Auckland Blues losing *again*, or the new restaurant they had tried on Saturday after reading a review in *Metro*, or even the Netflix documentary they'd been watching all Sunday afternoon. Instead, everyone was talking about a little accounting firm, down on the corner of Fanshawe Street and Victoria Park.

They were talking about us.

Now that the city was back to life, we were surrounded by more police cars, more orange cones, more yellow tape and more cameras. People wandered by on their lunch breaks, as close as they were allowed, just for an Instagram photo and a glimpse of the drama, down on that little end of town that nobody ever went to. If you had asked any of us in our wildest of wild dreams if we thought being an accountant would somehow bring us fame, we would have called you a fool. And we would've been right. Because here we were, the most popular news story in the country, maybe the world, and still nobody knew our names. Nobody knew our faces. Nobody even knew we were here.

From the moment we woke up that morning, Chocolate was back to being the group's news anchor. While Sienna laid out a breakfast of raisins, canned pineapple, bagels, and water in empty wine bottles, Chocolate cycled through every newspaper he could find, reading the headlines aloud, proudly, like he'd written them himself.

New Zealand Police claim to know identity of shooter.
Chief of Police refutes claims of mishandling "complicated" shooting situation.

New Zealand reeling from racial attack at popular Persian restaurant.

Siege continues for third day at prominent New Zealand office tower.

Steven Black rolled his eyes. "Bit of a stretch calling our building 'prominent', don't you think?"

I smirked. "What are they supposed to say? Shooting at... a little office building in Auckland? That nobody's ever heard of?" Sienna glared at me, and I laughed, sucking on a pineapple cube. "Why are these so sweet, anyway? Do they put sugar in them or something?"

"They're in syrup."

"Ahh." I took another one, balanced it on a piece of bagel and popped it into my mouth. "How long you think before we lose the front page spot?"

Darsh looked up from his laptop, thinking. "Probably depends if we die or not. If we die, we'll be front page for a week. If not, the All Blacks will probably get our spot before then."

"They're playing this weekend, right?"

"I think so."

"I wonder what pictures they'll use of us. Better not be our GW mugshots."

"Oh, man!" Chocolate laughed. "My one's terrible."

"So is mine," Steven Black said, battling with a mouthful of bagel.

"I think what they do now is they go into your Facebook and find a good one of you," Sienna said, finally sitting down to eat. She slid over next to me and grabbed a bagel from the bag.

"Better tidy my one up, then," Chocolate said, swiping on his phone.

"Don't post anything stupid," Sienna warned. I'd noticed she'd become more motherly these past few days.

"Just gonna delete the drunken ones. I want New Zealand to know I was a good Christian boy with a nice smile."

We giggled at the silliness of it. Like he was choosing his funeral photo. Then, after a few more bites of bagel, we all started doing the same, realising it might not be so silly after all.

With the help of six or seven bottles of red wine, the day once again passed in a flash. Superintendent Delowe only called twice during the day, with the usual disappointing update we'd gotten sick of hearing. *We're working around the clock. We'll have you out of there soon.* One of his calls we'd almost avoided answering until Darsh – the voice of reason – pulled himself to his feet and grabbed my phone from the lunchroom bench. In three short days, this had somehow become our new normal; living on junk food, alcoholism, walking on tiptoes, whispering every time we spoke. Steven Black had also made a winning discovery – two bottles of whiskey and a dozen beers in the boardroom fridge, which was disappearing quickly. By the time night fell, even he was struggling to finish a beer.

"Truth," Steven Black said.

"Again…?"

"What's wrong with truth?"

Darsh rolled his eyes. "We need to have a rule, man, like if you say truth three times, your next one has to be a dare."

"That's a South Auckland rule, bro."

Chocolate and Darsh both giggled, and Steven Black laughed drunkenly, loud enough to be heard on the floor below. We scowled at him, and Chocolate, also long lost to the whiskey, picked up an unopened beer can and threw it at him. Steven Black dipped his head, and I winced, Sienna cupped her hands over her mouth, Chocolate said "Ooh!" and we all watched it zoom past Steven Black's ear, hit the floor with a resounding thud, then roll painfully loudly along the wooden floors almost to the door.

Finally, it hit the wall and clunked to a stop, the trail echoing so heavily we clenched our jaws and sat frozen, silent, as if waiting to hear a barrage of terrorist footsteps clambering up the stairs.

"Gonna get us killed, nigga…" Darsh said, rubbing Chocolate's shaved head with a violent scrub.

"Yeah, nigga," Steven whispered.

"Steven!"

"What?"

Sienna glared at him. "You're not allowed to say that."

"Why?"

"Because you ain't black, nigga," Chocolate said, laughing.

"Neither are you!"

"Dude, my name's Chocolate. How much blacker could I be?"

Darsh laughed, holding out his hand. Chocolate slapped it, and they grinned at each other.

"That's ridiculous. Neither of you two are black," Steven said, scoffing.

"Look at me!" Darsh rolled up his sleeves. "I'm blacker than Tupac."

"Well, Chocolate ain't," said Steve, laughing. "Chocolate is peanut butter."

"Pssht, mate. I'm at least blacker than Obama."

"You're about the same," I said, laughing.

"Yeah, so if Obama says it, I can say it too."

"Obama never says that word," Sienna said, still serious.

"Man, I bet when Obama's in the shower, he screams it. He said he loves Biggie. So you know when he's in there scrubbing away, he's ripping it! *If you don't know, now you know, nigga.*" He bopped his head as he sang it, and Darsh joined him. And for some reason it was the funniest thing in the world, even Sienna couldn't help but laugh.

"When did that become a bad word, anyway?" Chocolate put the bottle to his mouth, gulping down wine like it was mineral water.

"It's only bad in America," Steven said.

"We used to say it all the time as kids." Chocolate shrugged. "They never even censored it on the radio."

I nodded, thinking back to primary school, when we all used to play *Ice Cube* on our Walkmans, and none of us understood a thing he was saying. "I didn't even know it was a bad word, until I was like, fifteen. In the movies, everyone said it to everyone. I just thought it was how you greet friends in America. You know, like how Samoans say *uce*? Then that famous lady said it on TV and lost her job. I was like, wait, it's a bad word?"

"Strange place, America."

"Is it a bad word in Europe?"

"No idea."

"What about Africa?"

"Dunno."

"Do they speak English in Africa?"

"Yeah, haven't you seen all those South African rugby players? Talk perfect English."

"But that's white South African people. What about black South African people?"

We all thought about it silently for a moment.

"I reckon they have their own native language. You know, like their version of Maori."

"Yeah!" Chocolate said. "For sure they do." He pulled out his phone and started searching. "The most common language spoken as a first language by South Africans is Zulu. 23 per cent. Followed by Xhosa, 16 per cent, and Afrikaans, 14 per cent. English is the fourth most common first language…"

"Alright, enough Wikipedia," said Steve. "Whose turn is it?"

"Yours."

"I said truth!"

"Okay, fine. I'll give you one," Darsh said, sitting up. "How many GW girls you slept with?"

"Dude."

"Oh my god." Sienna covered her face.

"You said truth," Chocolate said with a shrug, gulping more wine.

"And you took the oath," I said, giving him a wink. I had my own bottle of wine and sipped on it as well.

Steven Black looked at each one of us. But looked especially long at Chocolate. He opened his mouth, silent for a second. Then spoke.

"One."

And we don't know if it was the answer, or Steven's face as he said it, but we all burst out laughing as quietly as we could. Sienna cringed, her hands still over her face, and Chocolate was now on his back, kicking his feet in the air. I just smiled.

"Who was it?" asked Darsh.

"That wasn't the question."

"Bro. We all gonna die soon anyway."

"I reckon Amy," said Chocolate.

"Me too," I said.

"Me three," said Sienna.

"Fuck off bro…"

"Well, who else would it be?"

"Is she in the rat-pack?"

Steven Black smiled. He was a terrible liar.

"Oh dude, then it could only be one person!" Chocolate laughed.

Steven laughed back at him and shook his head, and Chocolate pointed at the sky, laughing wildly like he'd solved the Da Vinci Code.

"Who?" Sienna looked at me and mouthed it silently. "Who?"

I shook my head. Not because I didn't know. Just because it still felt like Steven Black's secret to tell.

"Since we're all gonna die anyway," Chocolate said, recomposing himself. "I'll tell you a secret." He took a deep breath. "I slept with her too."

Steven Black's mouth dropped. "I knew it!"

"Oh god," Sienna mumbled.

Darsh was now finding it hard to breathe between laughs. Sienna's face had been out of her hands for just a few seconds, but she sank it back in to hide her smile. Chocolate and Steven Black were in their own world now, both rolling with laughter, both drunk, and not looking like they'd stop any time soon. Sienna left to go toilet, and I left to get another drink.

When she came back, I was sitting on the floor by the fridge with a Coke and a fresh bag of pretzels. Chocolate had started falling asleep. Darsh was on his phone. I had no idea where Steven Black was.

She sat down beside me. "Who were they talking about?"

I sucked on my bottom lip, wondering if I should say anything. But they were probably right. We were all gonna die soon. "Well, there's only two girls in the rat-pack, and one of them rarely stays to go out. She usually leaves before you. So work it out."

She thought for a while, then mouthed the name silently.

I nodded.

"Oh. But doesn't she have a boyfriend?"

"Apparently."

She lifted her eyebrows and sat against the wall next to me. "I guess she is always hanging around you boys."

"Yep. Anyway, it's your turn."

"My turn?"

"Truth or dare."

"Oh."

She took my Coke and took a sip. And then another, longer one. Then she swapped it for the pretzel bag.

"Truth."

I didn't know why I had asked her to keep playing. I didn't have any questions for her. At least none that I thought I needed an excuse to ask. But I did have something I'd been thinking about.

"Okay… you know how, sometimes you meet a girl, and say she's learning French, right, or German, or whatever."

She glanced at me sideways, wondering where this was going.

"And then you ask her, why you learning that? And almost every time she'll say she's doing it for, I mean she might not admit it straight away, but every time she's doing it because…"

"Of a guy."

"Yeah!" I laughed. "See, even you know."

"Yeah, and what's wrong with that?"

"Wrong? Nothing's wrong with it. The opposite, actually. It might be the best reason to learn a language – so you can talk to someone, or love someone, or whatever. What would be a better reason? So you can get a better job? So you can go be an accountant in Germany or something? Fuck. That."

She snorted with laughter, and a bit of Coke ran down her chin. "You're such a hater. I mean, most people don't love this job… but you…"

"Anyways, the question is, was that the same for you? Like with your drama school, plays, and all that? Was there some boy you liked back then, and he acted or something, so you went and got out *A Streetcar Named Desire* from the library? You know, so he'd notice you?"

"Interesting theory."

I shrugged. "I mean, playwriting. I was thinking about it. You're the first person I ever met who talked about plays as like a hobby, or a job, or I dunno. As anything."

She pulled a handful of pretzels from the bag and started eating them one by one, chewing as quietly as possible as if the crazies downstairs could hear the crunch.

"And you're also the first person to eat your pretzels whole. Like, you're supposed to bite them first, man. What the hell?"

"What? But they're so small."

"Look how they're made! They're separated into little sections for you. You're obviously supposed to bite each bit on its own. See that part, bite that first, and then you get a little stick there, bite that off. It's like an Oreo. There's a proper way. You don't just put the whole thing in your mouth."

"It's not even close to an Oreo!" She glared. "Each part of the Oreo tastes different. This whole thing tastes the same." She waved one in front of me before placing it in her mouth, theatrically this time, the whole thing, as always.

I shook my head. "Such disrespect to the pretzel inventor. He'd be rolling."

She grinned, satisfied. "But no, it wasn't."

"Wasn't what?"

"A boy."

"Oh."

We both fell silent, and I looked across at her. I noticed how oily her hair looked. Freckles on her face

I'd never noticed before. Three studs up on the top of her left ear I'd never noticed before. She didn't seem to mind or even notice I was looking at her, so I didn't stop. Slowly, her mind drifted away. I could see it, like those times when you're staring at something, anything, it could be a plant or a latch on a window, but you're not even seeing it. Your mind is just away, painting a memory of something else.

"How much longer, do you think, until we get to walk under that night sky again?" she whispered, nudging her eyes toward the window.

I turned and followed her gaze to the sky outside. I always dreaded it in winter, but now, I missed those long walks back to my car in the evenings. Especially the winter ones, where the bite in the air left your cheeks chilled like ice packs, and you shivered as you climbed behind the steering wheel and cranked the heater up to high.

"I don't know, but for one long breath of fresh air... I'd give every last dollar in my bank account."

She looked over at Chocolate and Steven Black, now snoring beside each other. Darsh had fallen asleep too, sitting upright in the corner. Then she looked back at me.

"You wanna do something stupid?" Her eyes were brazen, but alive. I stared into her pupils, beaming right back at me. But I didn't say no. That was all she needed. With newfound zest, she rose to her feet, grabbed her sweater and tiptoed towards the door. As I watched, confused, and wondering if I should follow, she looked back at me, cupped her hand around her mouth, and pointed. "Bring the pretzels."

I rushed after her down the hallway, all the way to the elevators. She was up on her tiptoes, peeking around the corner into reception like somebody might be hiding, waiting for her.

"Stay here," she said softly, resting her palm on my arm. Then she pulled her sweater on, like a cape (it was black), dropped to all fours and crawled towards the reception desk.

I couldn't guess what she was doing. Fetching something, obviously, but what? Then, as she crawled behind the desk, I flinched, ready to scream as I listened to the painful creak of a drawer opening. She was now right in front of two huge windows opening out onto Victoria Park, in full view of anyone down below who might be looking, and suddenly I understood what she meant by 'something stupid'. But she was only there for seven or eight seconds before she started crawling back. Even then, all she seemed to have was a stapler in her hand, and a splatter of sweat dripping down her forehead.

"What the fuck!"

"Hey, I did it for you."

"For me!?"

"One long breath of fresh air, right?" she huffed, pulling a set of keys from her pocket. "And it won't even cost you a cent. Let's go."

Nothing made sense. No windows were able to open in office towers. It had been that way for years. That's why the air conditioning was always on. I guessed she was finally going a little crazy. One of us had been bound to, eventually.

Before I could ask questions, she was back on her knees and crawling again. I followed her, this time to the door to the stairwell.

"We can't open that!" I whispered.

Without breaking eye contact, she grabbed the handle, slowly, and pushed it down even slower. It squeaked loudly, and I pressed my eyes shut and gritted my teeth, somehow thinking that would make it quieter. Then she nudged the door with her hip, ever so softly, until it broke from the frame and cracked open.

"Sienna, fucking stop, Jesus. The card system is off. If we go out there, we can't get back in."

She held up the stapler and blew a kiss playfully in my face. Then she pushed the door open a little wider, stepped out, and held the door open for me to follow. As I did, I could feel my stomach drop through the floor, my heart thumping so fast I could feel the pounding down between my toes. As she eased the door shut, she wedged the stapler in the door frame, so it wouldn't shut completely.

"We can't be too long," she said, grabbing my hand.

I looked down the stairwell, expecting to see bombs, bullet holes, shells, something. It was like stepping out into the jungle, naked, where danger lurked in any direction. My feet trembled, and I shuffled, rather than taking proper steps, scared someone might see or hear us. Had she not had a hold of my hand, pulling me along, I'd have turned around and rushed right back to safety.

We tiptoed past the toilets, and just a few metres along there was another door I'd never seen before. It was smokey grey, the same colour as the walls, and blended in seamlessly. Obviously, it had always been there, but when in the stairwell there was never any reason to walk further than the toilet door, so I never had.

Sienna pulled the keys from her pocket, fit the key into the lock with a *zoink* and pulled the door open. Behind it stood a narrow hallway with nothing but a long stretch of stairs going up, a couple of storeys at least. All I could see at the top was another door with a small window. And moonlight. It was the way to the rooftop.

She cradled the door shut behind us and we climbed the stairs as quietly as possible, but swiftly. As we reached the door at the top, I pressed my fingers against it. My heart jumped twice. This was all that stood between us and the world outside. She fiddled with the key and slotted it in, less mindful of being quiet this time, cranked it sideways and pulled the door open.

My knees buckled as the first surge of wind swirled against my face. I held my palms out, not sure if it was real, the night air almost choking me as I breathed in gasps, faster and deeper, afraid it might run out or disappear. I'd never seen the night sky so velvety, so thick. So *near*. Only a few stars were out, but they had never been brighter or more beautiful. Sienna grinned as she watched me, then stepped out onto the rooftop and spun around, her arms outstretched like a toddler dancing in the rain.

***

"Remember when you told me you didn't know what a play was?" she asked, putting another pretzel in her mouth.

For some hours, we'd been sitting up against one of the metal vents in the centre of the rooftop. It was the deep of the night now, and the cold was starting

186

to bite. Though we hardly minded it. After four days inside that lunchroom, we would've stayed sitting out there even in a hailstorm. She laid her sweater over our knees.

"Well. I have a confession." Her gaze stayed fixed as she talked, staring out into the distance. So did mine. It was like every time we looked upward, we couldn't peel our eyes away. I'd never imagined I could miss the sky so much. "I didn't know either. What a play was. I thought I did. But I didn't. At least not in the beginning." She ate the last pretzel in her hand, then dusted her palms off against each other. "You know what the first play I saw was?"

I didn't say anything. Just looked at her.

"I was eleven, my cousins were in town, and we decided to go to the theatre. We'd never been to the theatre, but my mother thought it would be good to take them somewhere. So we went to this play. It was called *A Raisin in the Sun*. And I thought I knew what a play was, but we got there, and there was this lady up on the stage. She had on this bright sunflower dress. It was like watching a movie, but it was real life. And she was so passionate and real, and I remember I didn't even really know what was happening, but I looked to the side of me and everyone in my row was… they just couldn't move. They were enchanted or something. Then in front of me, a woman was crying. That's when I realised, people come to plays to see things and hear things you can't hear anywhere else, not on TV, not in the movies. It's a different kind of power, you see up on the stage. I just remember thinking; I want to do this. I'm not much of an actress, but I want to do this, I want to make something like this. I want to make something people love this much."

"A Raisin In the Stars?"

"A Raisin In The Sun."

"What's it about?"

"Maybe you should read it."

"Yeah, I will." I meant it, too.

"Anyway, it's your turn."

"My turn?"

"Truth or dare."

"Oh!" I rubbed my hands together and breathed into them long and deep. They felt like ice packs.

"Dare."

She screwed up her nose like she'd wanted me to say something else.

"Okay. I dare you…" Her voice trailed away, and she rolled her eyes playfully. Left, right. As if she had two options in her mind and was scrolling between them like a multiple-choice question. "Here's my dare. I dare you, when we get outta here, to go to the

Civic, put something nice on, some nice clothes, all that, and go watch whatever play is on that weekend."

"Yeah, sure. That's easy."

"And you have to take a friend. Someone you haven't seen in a long time."

"What, like from high school?"

"Anyone."

"Okay…" I took a second to think, but nobody obvious came to mind. "But why?"

"Because when you see a play, it's an experience, and that experience becomes a memory. If you share it with someone, especially someone you don't see often, it becomes a lasting one. Like my cousins. Even now, ten, fifteen years later, they still talk about it – *remember that night? The night we went to the play?*"

"I'll take Sam Drewlove."

We both closed our eyes and cackled together, extra joyously, as we could laugh normally now. The sound drowned in the wind. Nobody could hear us for a thousand miles. As another gust blew past, she linked her arm with mine and shuffled closer, laying her head on my shoulder. Her hair brushed against my cheek. Somehow, it still smelled of expensive shampoo.

"I mean, I'm gonna say yes, obviously. I'll do your dare. But you know what's gonna happen, right? All of us have been sitting here, talking about how 'when we get out of here we're going to do this, we're going to do that.' It's all bullshit. Like when someone you love dies, and you start saying 'Life is short! I'm going to make a change! Life is going to be so different!' And it is, for two weeks. Then you forget about it all and everything goes straight back to the way it was." I crumbled a pretzel between my fingers and watched the dust sprinkle on the floor in front of me. "Things don't change that easy. When I'm back at my desk and you're back at your desk, and all this is over. We're going to forget all these conversations. Just like we forget every other conversation. And life is gonna go right back to the way it was."

Tuesday

Chocolate came storming into the lunchroom. He couldn't shout, obviously, but you could tell he wanted to. He was so close to blowing, if someone just flicked his shirt, or looked at him the wrong way, he wouldn't have cared if the crazy man downstairs heard every word. He would have screamed the whole building down.

"They know."

I was still only half awake, barely conscious enough to reach and grab my water. Steven Black was sitting with his knees up, staring at the floor. Darsh and Sienna were still sleeping.

"What do you mean they know?"

"They fucking know, man! It's on the front fucking page!" He held his phone screen up, and I crawled up close enough to read.

BREAKING: Several staff trapped inside Grant & Woodson Tower, hostage situation likely.

"Oh fuck…"

Sienna's eyes opened, obviously sensing the nervousness. She saw the look on my face and sprang up. "What's wrong?"

I hesitated a moment. "They know."

"What do you mean, they know?"

I pointed at Chocolate's phone. She crawled up to him and read it.

"Oh fuck…"

"The only way they could know is if someone told someone."

I shook my head quickly. "I didn't say shit."

Sienna shook her head. "Me neither."

We stole a glance nervously at each other, but for a split second and no more. We knew what had happened. Someone had seen her crawling behind the reception desk. Or someone had seen us on the roof. My heart sank as I replayed the night in my head. It was so stupid. *Of course* they saw us. This was the biggest story in the world. How could we have been so stupid?

By now Darsh had woken up too. "What's going on?"

Everyone ignored him. We were staring at Chocolate, his face boiling.

He slowly turned to Darsh. "They know."

"What do you mean, they know?"

He held up his phone again, and Darsh poked his head forward to read it. "Oh, fuck …"

"Steve?" Chocolate said.

Steven Black's head was hanging between his knees. He looked up, shook his head. "Didn't say nothing."

"You're the fuckin' worst liar in history. I saw your face when I walked in. Who the fuck did you tell?"

I couldn't let Sienna take the blame. I'd say it was me. I'd say I got drunk and walked past the window. Then, just as I was readying to open my mouth, I caught Steven Black look nervously back at Chocolate, then at me, then at Sienna. He took one deep breath. And then it was as if he knew there was nowhere to hide; that he couldn't hold in whatever secret he had any longer.

"I just thought my dad might …"

"You're fucking joking…" Chocolate fumed.

I'd never seen him angry before. His face was so red, you could feel the heat coming off it.

"Look, I just thought my dad can pull some strings and get us out of here, okay? And I bet it wasn't even him that leaked…"

"Pull some strings! What the fuck kind of strings, bro? Are you fucking retarded?"

Steven punched the floor and sprang to his feet. It was like he bounced across the room in two steps, suddenly his face just inches apart from Chocolate's. "I'm not dying in this fucking place, okay!?"

"What, you think your daddy's money is going to buy a SWAT team to come flying in here? Your daddy can't do shit except get us killed even faster, you dumb ass white boy!"

"My dad knows exactly who to call, and the police downstairs aren't doing jack shit! So I told him, yes, okay! Police don't do shit, and none of you idiots did shit! So you dumb ass niggas should be thanking me for…"

Bang.

It felt like I heard it before it even happened. Even louder than the gunshots we'd heard on that first day. It was like he moved so fast, the floor shook, and everything moved in fast forward for a moment. I looked first at Chocolate's fist, no longer clenched, but shaking. Then at Steven Black on the ground, holding his cheek. Then at Sienna's hand gripping my arm, like she was on a roller coaster. Then at Darsh's face, his eyes larger than marbles, staring up at Chocolate. He stood there, his eyes fiery, staring through the floor. That definitely wasn't the first time he'd punched someone. But it certainly looked like the first time Steven Black had taken one. He ran his tongue over his lip, then spit out a blob of blood, twice, three times. Chocolate took another deep breath, stared at him for one more painfully long second, and walked out of the room.

Superintendent Delowe called barely five minutes later.

"Who did you tell? What did you tell them? When? Why? Where are you now? Have you heard anything from the stairs? From the elevator tube? From the windows? Stay off the phone! I'm gonna have to call you back."

I didn't know where Steven Black was. I didn't know where Chocolate was. It was just Darsh, Sienna, and me, sitting silently in the lunchroom. We were too afraid to move now. Too afraid to even speak. Now that everyone knew we were here, it felt like we were just waiting. Waiting for this building to blow up. Waiting for someone to come up the stairs to load that door with bullets. Any second now.

Then I pulled myself to my feet. It didn't make sense anymore, just waiting for our fate like this. "If this guy… if he's really just one guy… what are we doing? If he comes up those stairs, he can't kill all of us, can he? There's five of us!"

Darsh looked around the room. "Three of us."

"I'm serious. We shouldn't be sitting here like this, just waiting, right? We die fighting? No?"

Darsh scratched his head viciously, then looked up at me. "Okay. So what do we do, Batman?"

"I dunno. We make weapons and stuff. Have a plan. Smash him in the head with a laptop or something. That's better than just waiting to get blown up. Right?"

He thought to himself for a moment, nodding. "I guess so. Yeah."

"Alright, cool. You're in! GW Army. Let's go. Sienna?"

We stood there staring at her as she lay on the floor, curled in the foetal position. She looked up at us, unmoved. Then finally sighed at us both. "He has a gun, guys. Bombs. What do you want me to do?"

"Something! Anything! We'll figure it out. Turn this place into a fort. If he's gonna kill us, we'll make it hard for him."

She sat up and sighed again, pulling her hair into a ponytail before shaking it a few times and letting it fall free. "Honestly, all I want is a big box of chocolates and these bloody cops to come in here and get us already."

"Chocolates?"

"Yes, chocolates. A girl's best friend, chocolates."

Of course. I couldn't believe I hadn't thought of that yet.

"What? What are you smiling at?"

"I'll make you a deal. I'll get you the biggest box of chocolates you've ever seen. Then you join our army."

She smiled, sensing it was my turn to do something stupid. "Deal."

I marched out of the room, down the hallway. All the way to the East Side. At the first sight of windows, I dropped to my stomach, army crawling so fast my knees and elbows grazed through my shirt and pants. When I got to Korean Amy's desk, I ripped out her bottom drawer. It slid out easily. Pushing it in front of me, nudging it along with my head, I army crawled back towards the lunchroom. By the time I got back, my shirt was drenched and sweat dripped from my nose like a running tap. I was gone barely ten minutes.

"OH MY GOD!"

I stood over the drawer proudly as Darsh and Sienna rummaged through it.

"Whose is it?"

"Amy's."

"Oh my gosh, Amy. I love you."

I pulled one of the snacks out and handed it to her. "Here you go. Choco pie. It's like a Korean Mallowpuff." I grinned as she took it from me and examined it, the same way I'd done with my first one just a few days earlier.

She ripped it open and took a bite, then groaned with pleasure with tightly closed eyes. "You can't be *serious*." She pulled another box from the drawer, but this time, I snatched it back off her.

"Thisssss," I smiled, "Is Pepero. The most famous snack in Korea. Strawberry flavour too – that's the best one. But you only get it if you join the army."

She took another bite of her Choco pie and smiled brightly before plucking the box gleefully from my hand. "I'm all yours, Mister President."

Two seconds later, Steven Black and Chocolate walked in. It didn't look like either of them had been punched again. I guessed they'd been out by the double window, talking. But it seemed they were more than just back on talking terms. They were... smiling?

"Where the hell did that come from?" Chocolate gasped, rushing over to the snack drawer. "What is this? Chinese chocolates or something?" He ripped open a Waffle Mate and ate the first one in a single bite. "Yo! This shit is *serious!*"

Steven Black grabbed the packet from him and took one for himself, moaning with delight as he chomped on it noisily. "Dude. *Serious.* Whose is all this?"

"Mine," said Sienna, smiling.

"Amy's," I said, swiping at her.

"So, Stevey and I were talking," Chocolate began, his mouth still half filled with waffle. "He was right. We've been doing nothing. Instead of sitting around here drinking all day, we should've been getting prepared. I mean, he's probably only one guy, right? And there's five of us! He can't kill us all."

Darsh and I winked at each other, and just as I was about to speak, Sienna pulled a Pepero stick from the box, took a single bite, and looked at me. A dash of sass sprinkled across her face.

"That's exactly what I've been trying to say to these two!"

We were exhausted by sundown. With the elevators off, we concluded the only way to the floor was through the stairwell door. The one that looked like a nuclear bunker. The one Sienna had wedged with a stapler the night before.

Darsh and Steven Black spent the day building a barricade in front of it that resembled an obstacle course, with several tipped-over desks and shelves from the mailroom. I was able to climb over it with ease, but Steven Black claimed it would be 'way harder for a guy holding an assault rifle'. It garnered a laugh from us all, but we agreed with him in the end.

Sienna, Chocolate, and I spent the day collecting an array of weapons from across the East Side; several planks of wood, some cables we'd tied staplers to as makeshift ball-and-chains, a cricket bat and wickets from under Joel's desk, a golf putter and seven golf balls from Peter Mack's office, and a diverse collection of knives from Chef Margot's kitchen. Chocolate looked proudly at it all, laid out over the lunchroom floor. He picked up a golf ball, tossed it up and down in his hand. "When he comes through that door, just watch. While he's climbing over Steve's obstacle course, I'll blast this thing right through his skull." He lifted his front leg and winded up like a baseball pitcher. "He'll die instantly."

"You'll miss and hit the elevator," I said.

"Nah, he'll hit one of us," said Darsh.

"More like it will bounce off the wall and you'll hit yourself," said Steven Black.

"I bet he'll throw it so slowly the guy will just catch it and throw it right back," said Sienna.

"Ha ha," Chocolate's eyes simmered as we fell into fits of laughter. "Let's see if you're still laughing after I save all your lives."

The quiet jingle of my phone broke us up.

"Delowe," Sienna announced, grabbing it off the table beside her. We hushed, and she answered it, holding it up for us to hear.

"Everyone okay?" he asked. "Nobody gone crazy yet?"

"Far too late for that," Sienna said, eyeing each of us one by one.

"I hear you. As you've probably seen, the news is going wild about you. Everyone wants to know who you are, if you're safe, if you're suspects, where you are. We've been getting pressured to let them know, but we haven't given them anything. It wouldn't help our cause, much. Though we've decided this – you can tell your families now. We think… we owe you that much."

I peered at Chocolate. I caught him stealing a glance at Steven Black, who was looking at the ground.

"The only condition is you tell us who knows. And we'll talk to them too. Explain the situation, not to do interviews, that kind of thing. To keep it just between us."

We were all silent, talking with our eyes for a moment. Just between us. Then we hummed in agreement.

"The stakes have changed too, now that everyone knows you're up there. But we think he's definitely not leaving that ground floor. As soon as he does, we'll have the bomb squad all over him and our boys will be in position. That's a good thing. Just stay up there, stay far away. That's where we can keep you safe."

We heard someone call his name, and he muzzled the phone for a second.

"We've got some developments here. I'll call you again in an hour or so. Hang in there, guys."

We sat staring at our collection of weapons. It looked impressive, laid out like our own peasant's armoury. I snapped a photo of it. But despite all that work, it seemed like now we wouldn't ever have to use it.

"That's true, you know. If he comes up here, police are going to come raiding right in. He can't come up," Chocolate said, assuredly.

"How do they know if he's coming up?" I asked. "You can't see into the stairs from outside."

"They gotta have some SWAT level cameras or binoculars or something."

"Possibly."

"What? Nah, man, they don't have SWAT level anything," Steven Black grumbled. "That's why we've been stuck up here forever. If they had a real SWAT team, Colin Farrell would just come up here with a helicopter, smash this window open and pull us all out. Then this guy will blow all his bombs in desperation. We'd all go flying away while the building goes up in flames."

"Shucks, too much Hollywood, this guy. This is real life, bro!"

"If we were in New York right now, that's exactly how it would happen!"

"Nah, you see those school shootings in America? The cops just sit outside too, waiting for the guy to come out. Just like Delowe."

"Then how come those are always finished in one day?"

Chocolate pouted his lips, thinking. "Because they're not real terrorists. They're just schoolkids. They can't plan these things properly. This guy downstairs, he's an expert."

"Yeah, like the Taliban," I added. "They're experts. It's been like a million years, and they're still hiding away in those caves. All the best armies in the world still haven't beat them."

"Yeah, damn. That's true."

"So, this is a Taliban guy downstairs?" Steven Black blurted out. "We'll be in here forever! We're gonna grow old up here."

We all laughed at the thought.

"I'm marrying Sienna then," I said, shooting my hand up. "We'll live in Meeting Room Two."

"That means I gotta marry one of these two?" Chocolate said, laughing.

"Yeah, that's legal now, you know." I winked at him.

"True, alright I choose Darsh."

Sienna hooted with laughter.

"Stevey looks like you're growing old alone."

"I'll just have an affair with Sienna."

"In your dreams!" she snapped.

"How about you two have a daughter then?" He grinned, pointing at us both. "I'll marry her, Hugh Hefner styles."

"Ewww," Sienna wailed with disgust.

Chocolate was still playing with the golf ball. I picked one up myself, rolled it around on the floor between my knees. I didn't quite know how to say it, but it seemed like a good time.

"Guys, I've got a confession."

Almost in unison, they all stopped fidgeting and stared at me.

I could feel their attention, but I didn't look up. Just rolled the ball in a circle, listening to it purr, over and over. "You know how he said we could tell our families?" I picked the ball up and closed my palm around it. Then finally looked up at Chocolate in the eye. "I already told mine. I told my parents. A few days ago. Before Steven told his." Not knowing what else to say, I shrugged, apologetically. "I couldn't not tell them. I couldn't."

"What did they say?" Chocolate asked. I guessed he might be angry, but his eyes were soft. He knew my parents. They'd met a few times.

"They understood, you know. I told them not to tell anyone, and that I hoped I'd be safe, and I'd call them every day. And they understood. That it had to be secret. They understood."

"I also have a confession," Darsh said humbly. "I told my parents, too. And my wife."

"Wait, you're married?" I asked.

"Yeah."

"Since when?"

"A few years."

"Shit, dude. You're like the most unmarried married guy I've ever met."

"Why?"

"This whole time, you haven't mentioned your wife once."

"I talk about her all the time. To myself. In here." He tapped his temple. "It's a private thing, marriage. Love is a private thing. To me."

"Anyone else tell anyone?" Chocolate asked.

Sienna looked at him sullenly. "I told my dad. And my brother."

"Sheezus! I guess I'm the only one who cared about not getting killed up here!"

"Man, that was a fucking stupid thing for them to ask anyway," I said. "We can't tell our *families*? Really?"

"And besides, our families want us to live too, you know," Darsh said. "If you tell them it needs to be secret, they'll keep it secret. Obviously."

"Yeah… I guess so," Chocolate mumbled, the golf ball now hanging loosely between his fingers. "So, is your wife the one who makes all those nice lunches you have?"

I laughed at the question, as did Sienna. As did Darsh.

"Yeah, of course. She's the best."

"Damn, smells like it. Shucks. I hate eating lunch next to you. My shitty tuna next to your royal Indian food. Stacked all nice in those fancy steel lunchboxes."

"I'll ask her to make one for you next time."

"Really?"

"Sure, she'd love to."

"Me too bro!" I interjected.

"And me!" Sienna blushed.

Darsh smiled at us, surprised. "How about you all come over for dinner one weekend? Pratha loves to cook for people. It's her favourite thing."

We all moaned at the thought of it. Chocolate almost whimpered in agony, holding his stomach. I closed my eyes and raised my face to the ceiling, imagining the spread of freshly cooked rotis and dahl and curry chicken steaming on the dinner table. My stomach churned, loud enough for everyone to hear, and Sienna slapped my belly lightly and laughed with amusement. So many times we'd experienced the scent of Darsh's food wafting out of the microwave and through the lunchroom. We'd all wanted to try a spoonful. Just none of us ever felt entitled to ask. Now that we imagined it, it was pure silence, and none of us could stop salivating. If that was the only thing we got out of this disaster – a freshly cooked homemade Indian feast in Darsh's dining room – maybe, just maybe, it would all be worth it.

That night I fell asleep in my usual spot, on the red couch in reception, facing the double window. Luckily, I'd never had to fight anyone for that spot. The couch was about a centimetre shorter than I was, and Darsh, Steven Black, and Chocolate were all half a head taller than me. They found it far more comfortable to sleep on the carpet in the hallway, or on the long bench in the lunchroom. Only Sienna joined me in reception, usually sleeping on the yellow couch opposite mine.

Sienna always fell asleep before me, halfway through our nightly banter. I would spend the next few hours restlessly awake, staring at my usual spot on the horizon out the double window. It was always right where the harbour bridge hovered an inch above the skyline; that spot always shined the brightest, the way the lights funnelled through the tiny gap in the bridge panels. But that night, I fell asleep almost instantly. Perhaps it was due to our long day of army crawling up and down the East Side, searching for timber and cricket bats. But the sleep was deep and instant, and once again, I dreamed in 4K, and 3D, and five senses, the smells and sounds so rich I could have sworn I'd entered not a dream but another dimension. In this dimension, Sienna walked in front of me, and again I couldn't see her face, but I knew it was her, from the straightness of her hair, the shape of her legs, and the paleness of her skin. She carried something – a box – the same box from my previous dream, and I knew so because of the red stain on the side, the one I had guessed was jam from a jelly donut, or a squirt of tomato sauce. Then she turned around, and I saw the box was half open, the lid hanging loosely off to the side.

"Open it," she said.

"But I'm afraid."

"What do you think is inside?" she asked.

"I have no idea."

"Then what is there to be afraid of?"

She smiled, and now I knew for sure that splotch of red had been jam from a jelly donut because I saw some on her teeth before she ran her tongue across them and held the box up to me again.

I could see her eyes were fearless, and her smile was warm, which told me the box was nothing but a gift. She nodded peacefully as I grabbed the lid and pulled it off. Inside there were firecrackers. They hissed loudly and then went off even louder, *bang bang bang*, but she didn't move because she was unharmed, and I didn't move, as they gave me no harm either. We just looked at each other and laughed like children as they fizzled out between us.

"There's one left," she said, dropping her eyes.

I looked inside, and indeed there was one lone firecracker left sitting inside.

"Take it."

I reached in and grabbed it, holding it out in front of me. It rumbled violently and burned to the touch, but it didn't hurt, so I didn't let go. And then it disappeared with a final *bang*.

My eyes opened so suddenly even the moonlight hurt them. I guessed it was about 4 a.m. I reached for my phone. As I sat up, I rubbed my face long and slow, twice, three times. It felt so good, for some reason. Then, peering through my fingers, I noticed Sienna's couch was empty.

I had vaguely remembered hearing her get up in the night, I presumed to visit the toilet. I peeped behind me at the boardroom door. It was still open.

"Sienna," I hissed.

Nothing.

Craving water, I shuffled into the lunchroom to fill my glass. The back bench was empty. Our usual circle on the floor was empty. As I made my way to the sink, I peered around the tables we'd stacked in the centre, and that's when I saw them. Darsh, Steven Black and Chocolate, all lying beside each other, surrounded by wine bottles.

"Chocolate," I whispered.

He didn't move.

"Chocolate!" Still nothing.

I threw a bottle top at him, and finally he stirred, staring at me with a single wrathful eye. "What happened? Something wrong?"

I shook my head. "Nah, just… sorry."

"Dick."

I quickly checked the meeting rooms, then went back to the couches and set my water on the coffee table. I rested my head in my palms, and as I stretched out the kinks in my neck, my eyes landed on Steven Black's obstacle course several metres away. It looked different.

I took another mouthful of water, then wandered over to look. It was hard to say if it had been fiddled with. Of course, the tables hadn't been perfectly straight to begin with, but when I got close enough to look, that didn't matter anymore. The door to the stairwell was ajar. And on the floor, jammed in the frame, was a black stapler.

A cold shiver crept down my neck, and suddenly my dream popped back into my mind, of Sienna and the box and the firecrackers, and it was like pieces of a jigsaw started to form in front of me, suddenly the dream made sense now, perfect sense, I don't know how I knew but I did. The red stain on the box wasn't jam from a jelly donut, or a drop of tomato sauce.

It was blood.

Aftermath

At 5:29 a.m. on Wednesday 24th August, we finally emerged from the Grant & Woodson tower. We were shielded from the media and taken straight to the police station, where we were reunited with our families. We spent some hours undergoing medical checks, gave statements, some questioning, and then were allowed to return home, returning for more questioning the following day. I stayed with my parents that night, and we ate the same corn soup I'd eaten so often during winters as a kid.

I didn't go to work the Monday the office finally reopened, or the day after, or the day after that. I didn't call in sick or send an email. Nobody called to ask where I was. Not even Sam Drewlove.

The days all moulded together. I spent the mornings waking up early, ironing a shirt, putting my suit on and driving to work. But I never made it to the office. Just parked my car, sat there for an hour or two and drove straight back home again. That was my way of feeling normal without having to be normal.

I didn't go to Sienna's funeral. I heard it was nice, and many people showed up. I just didn't feel ready to say goodbye at the time. I knew she wouldn't have minded if she was indeed watching.

Mid-week, the office did finally call. It wasn't Sam Drewlove. It was the HR lady. She said the firm was arranging counselling, optional of course, and that I could 'take as much time as I needed'. They understood this was a 'very challenging experience'.

Chocolate emailed me during the week. "Just thought I should check on you" was the opening line. I'd found it odd how all the boys were back at the office as if nothing had happened. And then I learned – they weren't. Darsh and Steven Black hadn't been seen. Chocolate was the only one. I suppose he was the only parent out of all of us. Maybe he was used to putting on the *everything's okay* face and getting on with it.

It was exactly thirteen days after the incident when I finally entered the Grant & Woodson tower again. I was emotionless as I stepped out of the elevator doors at reception. The first thing I saw was Sienna's replacement, a fifty-year-old British woman, sitting behind the reception desk. She seemed nice enough, but it jarred me to see her there, sitting in Sienna's seat, a big rosy smile on her face. I had imagined Sienna's seat would be retired, like a star player's jersey in the stadium rafters, or that her replacement might sit on the other end of the desk for a few weeks. Just as a sign of respect. And then I thought, no, of course not. That was silly. If you retired someone's seat after they died, there'd be no seats left after a while. She was just the receptionist, after all.

I went and said hi to Chocolate first, who seemed to be doing okay, and then walked straight into Drewlove's office. He was on a call, but he saw me and shifted in his chair quickly, like suddenly I was the most important person in the world at that minute – "Sorry Ann, let me call you back, okay?" – and jumped up to close the door behind me. I sat down.

"Sorry I haven't been in. It's just…"

"No need to explain. We know."

I stared at the ground for a silent moment, but it felt like he already knew what I was going to say. "It's just…" Shaking my head, I looked up at him quickly. He was staring at me, but his eyes were curious. He looked at me differently now. For once, he wasn't rushing like we were on the clock. For once, I was the most important person in that office. For once it was my job to talk, and his job to listen. "I don't know when I'll be able to… you know. *Be here* again."

He nodded but said nothing. Just looked at his screen and pressed a few buttons, perhaps just to break the silence. "Well, what's important to us is that you're okay. And you're healthy. You're an important part of this team. I want you to know that."

Even now, his voice had that little whip at the end. He always had to sound so diplomatic, like it was hard-wired into his vocal cords.

"Thanks," I said, almost whispering.

"Why don't you take the morning off, take a walk, have an early lunch? Gordon's covering your urgent jobs right now, so there's not much to catch up on. Come back in the afternoon, and we'll talk it over."

I went back to my desk and sat erect in my chair, feeling the split-second stares of everyone who walked past. I flicked through emails but couldn't escape the eeriness of Chocolate sitting on the other side of the shelf, working away as if nothing had happened. As if everything we had been through had simply been erased and forgotten. All I wanted to do was roll around to his desk and say to him, "She died, man. I saw the body. I held her. She's not coming back."

I wanted to know what he would say. I wanted to know if he thought about her as much as I did. I wanted to know if people had asked about her. If they missed her. If anyone had complained that there was already a fifty-year-old replacement at reception, sitting in her chair as if she'd never existed.

I reached over to my top drawer to get my bag of peanuts. Not that I felt like eating. I just needed something to do with my hands. But the second I pulled the drawer open, I froze. An orange piece of paper. It was folded neatly into a square, sitting on top of everything. My stomach shook when I saw it, and for some reason, my first instinct was to look around to see if anyone was watching, as if I had discovered a looted bag of diamonds or a suitcase full of cash. I picked it up gently as if it were a hundred years old and might fall apart, and as I brought it closer to my face, I could see the shadow of writing inside. A letter.

I slipped it into the inside pocket of my blazer. Heart thumping, I walked hurriedly toward the bathrooms, the first place I could think of for privacy. But as I came into reception and approached the door into the stairwell, I halted violently at the sight of it. I felt the new receptionist behind me look up and heard the opening squeak of her voice, probably about to ask something like, 'Are you okay?' or 'Is something wrong?' but remembering who she was talking to, stopped herself and thought it better to stay quiet. I hit the elevator button instead – it was already on our floor so I wasn't forced to wait – and as soon as we hit the ground floor and the doors opened I rushed out into the park, where it wasn't raining, but the wind was damp and there was still the smell of leftover rain in the air.

Pulling the paper from my pocket, I already knew what was waiting inside. I didn't know how I knew, but I did, and as I opened the folds and saw the first words I recognised the handwriting, likely from all the Friday nights I had stood opposite her at that reception desk, looking at the sticky notes that collected up the side of her screen and across the top of her keyboard. To this day, I don't know if that letter made things harder or easier. But I do know, I wish I'd never had to read those words. I wish she could have spoken them to me, over pretzels on a Friday, across that reception desk. But maybe that's why they became the words that they did. The words I told you about. The ones that changed my life.

When I was five, maybe six, I was watching a movie with my brothers one night. My mum was there too. I couldn't tell you what movie it was, or what it was about. All I remember is there was a dead person at the end, and her eyes were open. I asked my mum, "If she's dead why are her eyes still open?" And my brother told me it was because there was a ghost inside her.

I asked my mum "Is that true?"

My mum smiled and shook her head, but she still didn't answer the question.

More than twenty years later, on that Tuesday night in the Grant & Woodson tower, I finally understood why. Because I was the same age as my mum was back then, and I didn't know the answer either.

That's the first thing I thought about when I saw Sienna's eyes, still open, glinting against the light of my torch. Once I saw them, I couldn't look away. They just drew my eyes back again and again. Because it wasn't the blood, or the way she lay, but the dullness in her eyes that told me she was never going to wake up again.

They spent almost three whole days questioning me down at the police station. Superintendent Delowe was around, but it was mostly Detective Greenlees I spent those days with. He asked a lot of questions. Why was I in the stairwell? Why was she in the stairwell?

"It was Tuesday night," I told him. "I woke up, I looked at my phone. I remember the time. 3:41."

He was scribbling furiously, even though I was being recorded.

"Sienna wasn't there. She'd been sleeping on the couch opposite mine, in the reception. I thought I had heard her go to the toilet, but that was hours ago. I looked out the window, saw all your cars and stuff. Nothing new. I figured, what the hell, I'll go look for her. This crazy killer guy isn't going to be awake at three in the morning. And we'd been becoming comfortable up there, you know? You stop being scared after a while. So I checked the boardroom, which was our toilet. She wasn't in there. Checked the lunchroom, wasn't in there. That's when I started feeling uneasy, like, maybe something had happened, but I couldn't guess what. Because if this guy had somehow found her and done something to her, surely he'd have found all of us, too."

"What about the others?" he asked.

I shook my head. "Everything was dead silent. All the boys were asleep. No sounds at all. All seemed normal. Well, not normal, obviously, but you know. So I came back to reception and saw the big barricade that Steve had built in front of the stairwell, and it just didn't look right. I went over and saw the door ajar, the stapler jammed against the frame. That's when I got this chill down my spine, like something had happened. Something not good. But after a second I tried not to think about that. I just told myself it's most likely nothing. She probably just went up to the roof again."

"And how often did she go up there before? Or any of you?"

"Just once as far as I know."

He nodded calmly, still scribbling.

"So I climbed into the stairwell. Then I crawled – literally crawled – towards the rooftop door, and by now I'm fucking terrified, but for some reason, I just didn't want to turn back yet. It felt wild to be out there alone, you know? And I looked around, and saw nothing, heard nothing. It was pitch black in there anyway, but I had my phone with me. That's all the light I had. I'm still crawling towards the door to the rooftop. I'm not even sure why I crawled. I probably would have made less noise just tiptoeing or something. And the whole time I was thinking, *terrible idea, terrible idea*, but I got to the door to the rooftop, and it was locked. So I thought, that's weird, if she's up there, shouldn't it be unlocked? But maybe it's one of those doors that locks on its own. I don't know. Anyway, I wasn't going to start banging and screaming for her to come let me up. So I just thought, okay, I'll go back. Then, as I'm crawling back, I shine my torch on the stairs down to the sixth floor. No reason, you know, just to look. And at the bottom, on the landing, that's where I saw her. I mean, I didn't even know if it was her... but I just knew it was her."

My voice croaked, and he stopped writing and raised his eyes at me. I looked back at him. As if we were waiting for each other to speak.

"Take your time."

I nodded.

"You need a drink or anything?"

219

"No, I'm okay."

"Hey, Jamie, get us a couple of coffees in here, please."

I looked over to the door and saw an old guy look at me and nod. I guessed he was Jamie. I looked back at Detective Greenlees. He did the straight-lipped smile.

"Just when you're ready."

Neither of us talked for a while.

"I crawled down to her. That's what I remember. I crawled down to her, and I don't know why, but I was relieved. I just assumed she was asleep. I was almost laughing, actually. Like, she really fell asleep in the stairwell with this wackjob just downstairs? It just never occurred to me that she could be... yeah. I almost took a photo. And I just whispered her name – *Sienna, Sienna* – and as I got closer, I could see the way she was laying. It was so unnatural, and then I put my hand on the ground next to her and felt it was damp. That's when I shone my phone up to her face, and I saw her eyes. I saw the blood on my hands. I looked down at her clothes, and there was blood all over them. I never saw so much blood in my life. And then I just looked back at her eyes, and I knew. I don't know how long I was there, thinking about what to do. I cried, I think. I'm not sure. I was in shock maybe. Is that what happens when you're in shock? But it was probably quite a few minutes, maybe even ten minutes, twenty minutes, I would guess. I don't know. And then luckily I heard all those footsteps coming up the stairs. I mean, it wasn't lucky right then because I thought, okay, I'm going to die now too. But luckily it was you guys."

"You were sitting there with her for about an hour."

"Really?"

"Yeah. Little under an hour. You would have heard shots, maybe some shouting a few floors down, doors opening and closing. You don't remember that?"

I shook my head.

He picked his pen up and scribbled some more.

What we hadn't known, what Superintendent Delowe hadn't told us, was CCTV was still working through the entire stairwell. He hadn't told us because he said until we could be questioned properly, we'd all been treated as suspects, too. When they'd seen Sienna and I go to the roof together, we'd even become 'possible accomplices'.

Once in questioning, they cleared us within a day. Detective Greenlees refused to show me the part of the tape where she was killed, but he did show me the part where they found me with her. He said he didn't mind doing so, since I had co-operated and everything I had told him 'lined up just fine'. It was odd to watch. I could barely recognise myself. Three or four officers came tiptoeing up the stairs, pointing guns at me, and I'd just backed up against the wall. There was no sound, and I didn't remember what they'd said. But from the tape, it looked like they decided pretty quickly I wasn't the guy they were looking for.

It was Superintendent Delowe who came in and shared the rest of the story. The shooter was a young man who had somehow gotten an access card for the building. That didn't surprise me; we used to lose our access cards all the time. After he attacked the Saturday gathering that morning at Pride of Persia, he holed himself in the building, but nobody knew what he wanted. Then after four days, he started moving.

"It was sudden, that night. He just armed himself up, started heading up the stairwell. We figured he'd do something erratic, eventually. Not sleeping, probably going crazy. CCTV had eyes on him, and as soon as he moved, we moved. We had bomb squad on that back entrance immediately, but they took a little while. And then in we came. Middle of the night. We're guessing he was trying to get to the roof. Not really sure why. Maybe to jump off, throw something off. You never know with these guys. But he got to your floor, saw your friend on the stairs and just…"

He paused. Rethought his words.

"It was dark, you know. I don't think he expected anyone in there. Definitely not a young girl. Once that all happened, it ruffled him a bit, we think. He tried for the roof, the door was locked. He came right back down, started barricading himself in the second-floor landing. We hadn't gotten that far yet. He had explosives, everything. All were duds, but the boys spent a long time trying to sort those out. And we had to clear every floor on the way up. Just protocol. That's why we took a little while to get to you."

I asked again to see the moment it happened. I felt like I needed to see it. But they wouldn't show me. 'Confidential' was the word they used.

"Was quick," he told me, after I pressed him for the third or fourth time. "She came down from the roof. He was coming up the stairs. He saw her and… just did it. Three, four shots. Really quick. Like a reflex." He spoke calmly, as if to soften it for me. "Even looked like he regretted it afterwards, when he saw who it was. Flustered him, we think. I can tell you, though, she would've gone instantly. Probably didn't even see him. Didn't suffer at all."

After we'd taken a short break, Detective Greenlees called me in for one last meeting. He had a folder in front of him, and his usual notepad, now covered in an array of neatly arranged notes and scribbles.

He set the notepad to the side and opened the folder. It was full of pictures. Small ones, like Polaroids.

"You recognise this guy, right?"

It was Chocolate.

"Yeah."

"You know him well?"

"Pretty well."

"How long you known him?"

"Three, three and a bit years."

"You think that's long enough to know someone *well*?"

I shifted in my seat, feeling discomfort for the first time. His tone had changed into something more calculating. "Are you trying to say Chocolate had something to do with this?" I asked, laughing. "You guys are insane."

"No, no, we're just... you know. Getting an idea of how you guys are all related."

I nodded sceptically.

"What about this guy?"

It was Darsh.

"Yeah, I know him."

"Works with you, right?"

"Yeah."

"You know him well?"

I looked doubtingly at him like it was a trick question. "Before, no. But now, yeah. I'd say so."

He scribbled a few words, then held up the next photo. "This guy?"

"Yeah."

"How well?"

I scratched my head, starting to feel impatient. "I don't know, I just know him, okay?"

"Spend much time with him?"

"Quite a lot."

"He ever say anything strange to you? Even jokingly?"

I shook my head slowly, thinking. "No, not really. Why?"

He held up another photo. "You recognise this car?"

"Yeah."

"Been in it before?"

It wasn't the best picture, but I knew those forest green panels anywhere. We all did.

"Yeah. Lots of times."

"When's the last time you saw it?"

And as he stared knowingly at me, he ignited my mind to run. There'd been so many memories in that car, but the most recent, I didn't know. I thought back to going for dumplings, for our long lunch on

Thursday, and seeing him bring it into the car park late on Friday night, and then… I wanted to say I'd seen it on Saturday morning, but I hadn't. Maybe it was the endless flow of beers we'd had that Friday night that had my memory fogged. But a replay of me walking past the car park played over in my mind. On the way back from the French bakery, the big box of croissants in my hand. As I'd walked past the car park, had I seen it? I had, I remembered it, vaguely. It was parked there, right in the back. Nothing would've looked odd about that. I saw his car in there almost every Saturday morning; I suppose that's why I'd glanced right over it. But now it struck me: Jeffery the Scotsman wasn't with us that morning. He'd driven home. Why was his car in the Grant & Woodson car park?

"But…"

Detective Greenlees put the photos away, pushed the folder to the side.

"Wait…"

Hiding a frown, he pulled his notepad back in front of him. Tapped his pen a few times. Looked up at me with sad eyes.

"You're trying to tell me that he…"

He nodded. "We need you to tell us everything you know about him."

It is a hard thing to be told you don't know someone you thought you knew. The idea you had of that person was a mirage, that something very different was hidden under the surface. All the conversations you had, were they real? All the laughs you shared, were they real? All the times they showed you kindness. Real?

Often, we assume people are good. We stand face to face with a stranger, having not yet known them for even a full minute, and we shake their hand. So many bad things could be done in that moment, but that never enters our minds. *What a nice guy*, we say. *So nice to meet you.* After one night, we may even consider them a friend. After a week, we may even invite them into our home for a drink, a meal, a conversation. But who is that person, really? As Detective Greenlees said, is three years enough to *really* know a person?

For all the years that followed, that was a question I would never stop asking with every person I met for the rest of my life. All because of him. All because of those four days.

We found out exactly one hour before the nation did. For the next few days, Jeffery Scott Docherty was about to become the most famous name in the country. Terrorist. Murderer. White supremacist. Demon. That was the hardest part. Seeing how other people talked about him. For the rest of our lives, we would wonder. What went through his mind? If we could have helped him. Why he had called us all that one afternoon, when none of us had picked up, not wanting to lie to him. Now it ate away at us, knowing he'd been just seven storeys below, needing us more than he ever had. But he was gone now. None of us would ever find out why he did it. What he wanted. Who was responsible for putting such a horrific idea in his head. That made it especially hard, and even harder to hate him like everyone else. It was reported later, though we only half-believed it, that he'd had some kind of personality disorder or drug issue, and a few other flimsy-sounding things. But we stopped paying attention to all that. We decided to remember him just as we knew him. We had to, for us and for him. It was the only way we could ever live with it, and ourselves. We only knew him as Jeffery the Scotsman, and we remembered him that way.

I quit my job a week later. There was no drama. Nobody dared to talk me out of it. I showed up in the morning, told them I couldn't be there any longer, collected my things and left. I told Chocolate we'd meet that Friday and talk things over. I said bye to Korean Amy. Gave a goodbye hug to Buck.

As I walked out through the car park, a tall, wiry man had just exited his car and was heading to the building entrance. He had a box in his hands. Looked like a cake.

I noted it was a nice car, jet black and small. It wasn't odd to see those kinds of cars in the Grant & Woodson car park, but it didn't stop you from noticing them and how expensive they looked. As I got closer, I caught a glimpse of the little silver jaguar shining on the bonnet.

Then I saw the number plate.

FINCH.

The man walked towards me, slowly, as if waiting for me to look at him. I did.

"Excuse me, young man. You look like an accountant." He laughed. "Grant & Woodson office, through here, is it?"

He was a vibrant man with perfect hair and young wrinkles. Large smile. Boat shoes.

I nodded at him. "Yes sir. Right through there." I pointed at the door behind me.

"Gosh, my wife would faint if she heard you call me that!"

"I'm sorry?"

"*Sir.* She cringes any time someone calls me that."

"Oh, right," I said, managing a smile. "Nice car, by the way."

He turned and gave it a little nod. "Yeah, she's a good little thing. It's my wife's car, actually."

"Oh yeah? Wouldn't have guessed. You're a client, are you?"

"Yes, sorry. Joseph. Joseph Finch."

We shook hands, and I introduced myself. "I recognise the name, actually. Sam Drewlove's client, right?"

"Yeah," he said, looking a little confused. "You work on my accounts?"

"No," I lied. "Just seen your files around the filing room."

"Oh, right."

"Yeah, how's business? What are you in?"

"My wife and I are both lawyers. I used to be her boss, actually." He laughed. "I'm retired now, but she... she loves it a bit too much. I said we already have plenty of money, but she can't stop, won't stop. Good for her, I guess. She's still young... ish."

I smiled politely. "And what keeps you busy, then?" I asked. "Another childhood in retirement? Playing some video games?"

"Funny you say that! I actually can't stand those game things. But tell you what, I feel like I should pay attention because it can't be a bad business to get into. My kids run up my credit card on this Xbox Live thing like crazy, you heard of that?"

"Yeah, had one a few years ago."

"Gosh, I thought you just bought the game, and that was it! But they seem to buy something new for it every darn day. They keep saying they're buying new levels or items or something. No idea how that works. No, for me, I just do a bit of fishing, cycling, that sort of thing. Get in the garden a bit."

"Yeah. That's nice. Good for you."

He paused for a moment, smiling hesitantly. "Say, I hate to ask but, how is it up there? After... that whole thing?"

I shrugged. "It's moving along."

"Yeah, I'm sure. I just thought I'd bring something in, to lift the spirits." He held up the box that looked like a cake. "My wife baked them."

"That's nice of you. I'm sure everyone will appreciate it."

We smiled at each other again, now both wondering how to say goodbye.

"Anyway, I've got somewhere to be."

"Yes, of course."

"Nice to meet you, Mr Finch."

As I exited the car park and passed the Pride of Persia restaurant, I noticed some of the yellow tape had come down. Police had been in and out of there most days, but now, I could see the doors wide open, and things being clunked around inside. I peered through the window and caught sight of the owner. I hadn't even known if he was still alive. I still didn't even know his name.

Don't let life go back to just the way it was.

I walked around to the front door and set my box of things on the floor. As I lifted my fist to knock, he caught sight of me first, and his expressionless face turned to a smile.

"Ah! Young gentleman! How happy I am to see you!"

I strode towards him, and we shook hands, then hugged. "I'm so sorry," I said as I pulled away, holding his shoulders under my palms. "I didn't even know if – I mean, I hoped but – your face wasn't in the newspaper. I guessed you…"

"I wasn't even here," he interjected. "I always leave early on Saturday to watch my boy play soccer."

We both held each other's shoulders, just looking at each other for a moment, feeling lucky. Feeling grateful. Like we'd known each other so well for so many years. In a way, we had.

"You know I've never asked you, all these years, what your name is."

"Kaspar," he said proudly, shaking my hand. "And you?"

I introduced myself. "And you're from Persia?" I asked.

He whooped with laughter. "I guess you could say that. Persia has been gone a long time. I am from Iran, my friend. It's the new Persia."

"Right, the new Persia. Got it. Well, Kaspar, I'm glad we finally met like gentlemen."

"Yes, of course. What's happening here?" he asked, pointing at my box of things outside.

I shrugged. "I'm moving on, I guess."

He looked happy for me. "And your friend?"

"No, he's still up there," I said, pointing upstairs.

"Well, I'll be open again, in a month or so, I hope. Don't forget to come back."

"I won't. I promise."

I savoured my final walk to my car, across the park and up the hill. Once I got there and placed my things in the trunk, I couldn't shake the feeling of lightness, of being in the city, in my suit and tie, but nowhere to go – no cubicle to go back to, no timesheet to fill, no urgent job to hurry back to the office to finish before five. It was overcast but warm, a sliver of sun managing to slip through the clouds. *This is what it feels like to be free.* It would be a crime to go home now, I thought, this newfound freedom beckoning to be enjoyed. I loosened my tie and headed downtown for a walk.

It had been years since I'd been downtown at that hour. It was near 11 a.m. There were a few young professionals wandering around, but it was mostly students, tourists, and retail staff on cigarette breaks. I bought a mocha from the most expensive cafe I could find and went wandering the city side streets; streets I hadn't seen or walked in years. Not far from the university, a young girl in honey-coloured overalls was battling with a long paint roller, pasting up posters for a Katchafire concert. She had short black hair and a frog tattooed on the back of her tricep.

"Cool tat," I found the courage to say as I walked past.

"Thank you!" she beamed, turning her head.

But as she did, I hardly heard her. My eyes had been drawn to another poster on the wall, a few metres down. I drifted towards it. In the centre was a woman in a yellow dress, surrounded by kids, and a tall, handsome man in a suit and a fedora hat.

As I studied it, captivated, my phone rang. My girlfriend. I answered.

"Hey, how did it go? You did it?"

"Yeah," I said. "Went fine. No drama."

"Wow, so now you're free! Are you happy?"

The poster was different from what I'd imagined. I'd imagined the sunflower dress Sienna had described on a white lady, probably homely looking, with lots of smiling faces, something like a Reese Witherspoon movie. But it wasn't. It was an African

234

American family, sitting around a dinner table, all dressed flawlessly, probably fresh from church.

I ran my fingers across the words along the bottom. *A Raisin In The Sun*.

"Hey? You there?"

"Yeah, yeah. Sorry."

Now showing. Civic Theatre. Tickets on sale now.

"You okay?"

"Yeah, I'm actually uhh. I'm kind of busy tomorrow. I promised a friend from work that I'd make time to do something."

"Oh. Okay. Well, the next day then?"

"Yeah. Perfect."

I hung up the phone. A bit abrupt, but it didn't bother me at that moment.

Don't let life go back to just the way it was.

I had a promise to keep.

The next morning, I didn't iron a shirt. Didn't put on a suit. Didn't fumble through my drawer for a matching pair of cuff links. But I still woke up at 7 a.m. and made my way to the city.

On my morning walks to work, there was a small stone fence that lined the block just beside the bookshop. All those mornings I'd walked past it, I'd never noticed it before. But I got there at fourteen minutes past eight, and sat there while I waited, nervous, maybe excited, maybe confused. Laughing in spurts, just at the thought of it. Or maybe at a sad realisation that *this* would be the craziest thing I had ever done in my life.

She was early that day. I recognised her shoes first. The brown ones, with the thick white soles. She wore them in the summer months, usually. Then the red satchel. And of course, the long auburn hair.

She noticed me from a distance this time. I guess because I stood out in my jeans and sneakers, and faded sherpa jacket.

"No work today?"

I laughed. "I resigned, actually." I stood up to greet her as she walked by. I wondered if she'd stop. She did.

"Oh yeah? Wow."

"Yeah. Just going back to pick up a few of my things."

"Good on you!" she said warmly. "I'm Natalia, by the way."

We shook hands.

"I always wondered what your name was all these years. My guess was something more like Zoe."

We both laughed.

I had never seen her up close before. Her hair wasn't actually auburn, but more of a copper brown, just like her eyes. Her face was sharper than I'd thought, Slavic roots perhaps, and her freckles stretched right up past her cheekbones to her temple. I tried not to stare, but she just looked so… interesting. I introduced myself.

"Listen, I'm going to ask you something, and it's really an odd question, so don't…"

"That's okay. I'd say I'm quite an odd person, so…"

"Oh?" I laughed nervously. And then became silent, thinking, for maybe a split second too long. "I had this friend… I mean, she's gone now, but… well I promised that I'd…" I'd run the script over in my head all morning, had memorised it perfectly, but now it was time to speak, I remembered none of it. "There's this… play."

"Play?"

"I know, it's kinda silly. There's this play, it's called *A Raisin In The Sun.*"

She nodded slowly, waiting to see where I was going.

"And… it's on right now at the Civic, tonight actually. I just wondered. Again, I know this is so weird. I just wondered, if you know, you'd want to go see it with me?"

"Me?"

I wasn't nervous anymore. It was funny now. She looked perplexed. I laughed. "Yeah. I wanted to take someone, and I thought. I dunno. I thought if I saw you today, I'd ask you."

She read my eyes for a few seconds, and slowly her squint morphed into a smile. "You're right, that was an odd thing to ask." She started laughing. "You said tonight?"

"Yeah." I nodded, more confidently this time.

"I mean…" She studied my eyes one more time, perhaps to see if I was joking. "Yeah. Yeah, that sounds fun. I'd love to."

She looked excited. I was excited. I laughed, again. I hadn't laughed in so many days.

"So… how do we do this? I'll meet you there? It starts at eight."

"Yeah, great. I just live down here, around the corner. I'll walk."

"I could walk you? If you want?"

Her face warmed as I said it. "That sounds nice."

I looked around. "How about we meet here?" I pointed at the bookshop. "Seven."

She looked it up and down, left and right as if she'd never seen it before. Then she nodded at me, her eyes coppery and soft like I'd never seen them before. "It's perfect."

I went home that night, and as I'd been doing every night, after dinner had been cooked, the dishes were clean, the heater was on, and I was about to get into bed, I opened the top drawer of my desk and pulled out the orange piece of paper.

Already the corners had blunted and wrinkled. I wondered how long it would be before the whole sheet looked like that, spotted with fingerprints and folds and accidental tears. How long before I stopped reading it? How long before it no longer meant anything? How long before everything just went back to the way it was?

I sat cross-legged on the floor and slowly unfolded it again.

I know the next play I'm going to write. It's going to be about an Australian man who is a rice farmer, and he moves to Cambodia (or was it Malaysia? I forgot!) and grows rice, and every season he sells some of the rice and then gives the rest away to poor people who have no money for food.

I'm going to write this play because someone once told me he wants to do something that matters to people, and I thought that was pretty cool.

Keep this as your little reminder, that when I'm back at my desk and you're back at your desk after this is all over, you don't forget our conversation like you forget every other conversation, and life won't just go back to the way it was.

Sienna x

P.S. Don't forget your dare! You promised.

The first tear hit my hand, but the second one fell onto the edge of the paper, and I watched it slowly spread into a tiny wet circle before I folded it back up and rested it between my fingers.

And then I cried. I cried so hard I almost scared myself at how hard my body cried. Heaving, I hunched over and ground my teeth and didn't let myself hold anything back. And then, as quickly as the crying had started, it stopped. I looked at the puddle of tears on my sleeve and huffed as I caught my breath.

"It won't," I whispered, smiling at her as if she was watching. "It won't."

About The Author

Brendan was born in Sydney, Australia and grew up in Auckland, New Zealand. After graduating from the University of Auckland, he had a short career as a tax accountant. He left New Zealand in 2011 to travel and pursue a career as a writer. He documents his travels on his blog, brenontheroad.com. His other books, *Iron Skin: A Memoir* and *The First $100K*, are available on Amazon.